The New York Times

IN THE HEADLINES

Transgender Rights

STRIVING FOR EQUALITY

EDUCATIONAL PUBLISHING
BOOKS

THE NEW YORK TIMES EDITORIAL STAFF

Published in 2019 by New York Times Educational Publishing
in association with The Rosen Publishing Group, Inc.
29 East 21st Street, New York, NY 10010

First Edition

The New York Times
Alex Ward: Editorial Director, Book Development
Brenda Hutchings: Senior Photo Editor / Art Buyer
Phyllis Collazo: Photo Rights/Permissions Editor
Heidi Giovine: Administrative Manager

Rosen Publishing
Jacob R. Steinberg: Director of Content Development
Greg Tucker: Creative Director
Brian Garvey: Art Director
Julia Bosson: Editor

Cataloging-in-Publication Data
Names: New York Times Company.
Title: Transgender rights: striving for equality / edited by the New York Times editorial staff.
Description: New York : New York Times Educational Publishing, 2019. | Series: In the headlines | Includes bibliographic references and index.
Identifiers: ISBN 9781642820645 (pbk.) | ISBN 9781642820638 (library bound) | ISBN 9781642820621 (ebook)
Subjects: LCSH: Transgender people—Legal status, laws, etc.—United States—Juvenile literature. | Sexual minorities—Legal status, laws, etc.—United States—Juvenile literature. | Transgender people—Legal status, laws, etc.—Juvenile literature.
Classification: LCC KF4754.5 T736 2019 | DDC 323.3'270973—dc23

Manufactured in the United States of America

On the cover: J Mase III, Poet. Educator. Founder of AwQward Talent, LLC. Damon Winter/The New York Times.

Contents

CHAPTER 2

Transgender Access Laws in Schools

Introduction

THE FINAL YEARS of the Obama Presidency marked a turning point in the lives of transgender Americans. For the first time in history, transgender issues moved from an offshoot of LGBT rights and into the spotlight. In 2016, Obama's White House ruled that students should be allowed to use restrooms that conform to their gender identity. The same year, the Secretary of Defense ordered for the acceptance of transgender service members in the military. Gavin Grimm, a transgender boy from Virginia, won national attention when he sued his school for preventing him from using the boy's bathroom. And dozens of television shows, films and books created by transgender artists featuring transgender stories have made their way into the mainstream.

These events have been matched by an increasing number of transgender Americans who have transitioned publicly. But despite these successes, the road ahead is long and hard. President Trump stated in 2017 that he would revoke protection for transgender service members, a position he doubled down on in March of 2018. Bathroom bills are winding their way through more state legislatures, and protections for transgender students in schools have been slipping. Violence against transgender men and women, particularly transgender people of color, continues, and, according to some reports, possibly even rising. Between a third and a half of transgender adults will attempt suicide at some point in their lives, and many more will experience bullying and harassment. And still, many states do not offer the protections against discrimination on the grounds of gender identity that are afforded to race and sexual orientation.

As in all civil rights movements, this one has its leaders. Among the most prominent are the voices of young people, from student activists to a generation of children and youths coming out to their parents and families. Journalists, celebrities and politicians have rallied together to highlight the need for change and to give voice to the thousands of individuals who identify as transgender, celebrating the diversity of transgender stories and fighting for their place in American culture.

This book features dozens of articles that represent the scope of The New York Times's coverage of the push for transgender rights. From opinion pieces to in-depth reporting, these pieces speak to The New York Times's commitment to covering transgender lives in a time of historical reckoning. This book highlights key moments in the fight for equality, from the Boy Scouts' acceptance of a transgender boy to the success of the television show "Transparent," as well as deep dives into issues that have marked the debate in recent years: transgender

RAY WHITEHOUSE FOR THE NEW YORK TIMES

A rally in Raleigh in April 2016 against a North Carolina law that barred people from using bathrooms that do not match their birth gender.

children in schools, bathroom bills and transgender service members. What emerges is a portrait of an evolving civil rights movement that honors the achievements of its leaders and sheds light on the terrain that still remains to be broached.

CHAPTER 1

Struggles in the Transgender Community

The struggle for transgender rights has been fought across various platforms: in culture, in the courts, in schools and in dictionaries. This chapter addresses some of the foundational problems and questions faced by the transgender rights movement as well as its historical underpinnings. From editorials about the future of transgender rights to reporting on the experiences of transgender Americans, this chapter shows the diverse range of challenges that transgender individuals face and the various inroads that have been made in the movement toward equality.

The Quest for Transgender Equality

OPINION | BY THE NEW YORK TIMES | MAY 4, 2015

BEING TRANSGENDER TODAY is still unreasonably hard, but it is far from hopeless. This is the first in a series of editorials looking at the challenges ahead.

A generation ago, transgender Americans were widely regarded as deviants, unfit for dignified workplaces, a disgrace for families. Those who confided in relatives were, by and large, pitied and shunned. For most, transitioning on the job was tantamount to career suicide. Medical procedures to align a person's body with that person's gender identity — an internal sense of being male, female or something else — were a fringe specialty, available only to a few who paid out of pocket.

Coming out meant going through life as a pariah.

Being transgender today remains unreasonably and unnecessarily hard. But it is far from hopeless. More Americans who have wrestled with gender identity are transitioning openly, propelling a civil rights movement that has struggled even as gays and lesbians have reached irreversible momentum in their fight for equality. Those coming out now are doing so with trepidation, realizing that while pockets of tolerance are expanding, discriminatory policies and hostile, uninformed attitudes remain widespread.

They deserve to come out in a nation where stories of compassion and support vastly outnumber those that end with a suicide note. The tide is shifting, but far too slowly, while lives, careers and dreams hang in the balance.

Many of the heartening stories have unfolded out of sight. Some employers in the public and private sectors have begun to openly support people making the transition. At the Central Intelligence Agency, a young analyst who transitioned on the job in 2013 worried that coming out would end her career. She realized that fear was unfounded when colleagues got her a gift certificate to Ann Taylor after she transitioned at work and senior agency officials made it their mission to ensure she could continue to thrive at her job. Yet at the same time, thousands of American troops who are transgender serve in anguish because the military bans openly transgender people from joining the service. Those who take steps to transition can be discharged under the current rules.

In several states, transgender people are courageously battling efforts to bar them from using public restrooms. In West Virginia, transgender women have been at war with the Division of Motor Vehicles because officials are refusing to give them new licenses unless they stop "misrepresenting" their gender when they have their photo taken. A recent federal government survey found that one in five transgender people reported having been denied care by a health care provider as a result of their gender.

These indignities and abuse account for the alarmingly high rates of homelessness, unemployment and suicide for transgender people. Leelah Alcorn, a 17-year-old from Ohio, wrote a harrowing suicide letter before leaping in front of a tractor-trailer last December.

"The only way I will rest in peace is if one day transgender people aren't treated the way I was, they're treated like humans," she wrote. "Fix society. Please."

Three years before a police raid of the Stonewall Inn in New York in June 1969 galvanized the gay rights movement in America, transgender women rioted after being expelled from Compton's Cafeteria in San Francisco. The restaurant had become one of the few safe gathering spots for the city's community of transgender people, who at the time were not welcome at gay bars. That same year, physician Harry Benjamin published "The Transsexual Phenomenon," a groundbreaking book that outlined how transgender people could transition medically. The two developments helped give rise to an arduous fight for societal acceptance.

Over the decades, the transgender movement has been part of the broader quest for equality for sexual minorities, but while gays and lesbians have achieved far-reaching legal and political victories in recent years, transgender people, who may be gay or straight, remain among the nation's most marginalized citizens. They face distinct challenges, including access to transition-related medical care, which have not always been a focus of the broader struggle for gay rights. Gays and lesbians are visible in all walks of life today, and many are celebrities and role models. Transgender Americans, meanwhile, remained largely unseen until fairly recently.

As prominent transgender people have come out in recent years, their revelations have been a source of fascination, much of it prurient. There was the actress Laverne Cox, the Army whistle-blower Chelsea Manning and most recently, Bruce Jenner, the gold-medal Olympian.

Their stories have brought attention to the plight of a segment of the population that continues to confound many Americans. One challenge lies in semantics, a complex and fraught subject given the extraordinary diversity of experiences within the transgender community. The term transgender covers a broad range of people who do not identify with the gender listed on their birth certificate.

Scientists have no conclusive explanation for what causes some people to feel dissonance between their gender identity and aspects of their anatomy. In 2013, the American Psychiatric Association updated its manual, replacing the term "gender identity disorder," with one that is less stigmatizing, "gender dysphoria."

The options for those who take steps to ease the distress has expanded significantly in recent years. Some opt to wear clothes typically associated with the sex they identify with, legally change their names and use new pronouns. Many also undergo hormone replacement therapy and have surgery to transform their bodies. Surgical procedures include chest reduction and augmentation as well as sex-reassignment surgery. Some people have just one type of procedure, others undergo both, and some choose to have none. While many transgender people identify with one gender, some feel their identity lies somewhere in between. The spectrum of experiences and identities is complicated, but taking basic steps to ensure that more transgender people lead healthy and fulfilling lives is not.

Expanded formal recognition is a fundamental first step. The size of the transgender community in America has always been unclear, since many people wrestle with gender dysphoria in silence. The most widely-cited figure, 700,000, comes from a 2011 study by the Williams Institute at the University of California, Los Angeles. The United States Census Bureau should give transgender Americans the chance to be formally recognized as such on forms, if they choose to.

Having more detailed information about the demographics of the population is crucial to the evolution of stronger legal protections and expanded access to health care. There has been significant progress on both fronts. Last year, Medicare, which has a big influence on the industry standard for insurance coverage, lifted its ban on covering gender reassignment surgery. More states and insurance providers are following that lead, heeding the call of medical experts who say transgender-related care must be viewed as "medically necessary," rather than elective.

There have been hard-won victories on the employment front, too. The Department of Justice last year began taking the position that discrimination on the basis of gender identity, including transgender status, constitutes sex discrimination under the Civil Rights Act. That memo adds to the growing body of case law and Equal Employment Opportunity Commission rulings that have strengthened legal protections for transgender workers. Yet, many jurisdictions lack local laws that protect transgender people and discrimination remains commonplace even in places that do.

President Obama has advanced transgender rights more than any American president. But there is a glaring form of discrimination that he has the power to end. The Pentagon continues to ban openly transgender people from joining the military, even though many of America's closest allies have integrated them seamlessly in recent years.

The lack of legal protections and access to necessary care in the military system has made thousands of transgender troops extraordinarily vulnerable. Some have been discharged for being transgender, while others have opted to quit, forgoing pensions and career advancement, because delaying their transition has become unbearable.

At the Department of Defense, a handful of senior officials have quietly met with active duty transgender troops to study how that segment of the force could serve openly. The officials have become convinced that lifting the ban would unlock the service members' unfulfilled potential. Defense Secretary Ashton Carter should ask these officials to lead a swift review of the steps the Pentagon needs to take to formally integrate transgender troops. While that review is underway, Mr. Carter should instruct service chiefs to stop expelling transgender troops who are in the process of being discharged.

A generation from now, scientists will most likely know more about gender dysphoria and physicians will undoubtedly have found better ways to help people transition. This generation should be the one that stopped thinking that being transgender is something to fear or shun.

Estimate of U.S. Transgender Population Doubles to 1.4 Million Adults

BY JAN HOFFMAN | JUNE 30, 2016

ABOUT 1.4 MILLION adults in the United States identify as transgender, double a widely used previous estimate, according to an analysis based on new federal and state data.

As the national debate escalates over accommodations for transgender people, the new figure, though still just 0.6 percent of the adult population, is likely to raise questions about the sufficiency of services to support a population that may be larger than many policy makers assumed.

"There's a saying: 'You don't count in policy circles until someone counts you,'" said Gary J. Gates, a demographer and former research director of the group that did the analysis, the Williams Institute at the U.C.L.A. School of Law, which focuses on law and policy issues related to sexual orientation and gender identity.

The Williams Institute is the research group that produced a widely accepted estimate five years ago. Its new number was drawn from a much larger federal database than it used to reach the earlier projection of 0.3 percent, or 700,000 people.

Noting that younger adults ages 18 to 24 were more likely than older ones to say they were transgender, researchers said that the new estimates reflected in part a growing awareness of transgender identity.

The analysis may also reflect the limits of self-reporting in obtaining definitive data. In some states seen as more accepting, more adults identified themselves as transgender. In some states perceived as more resistant, fewer adults did so, even though the surveys were anonymous.

The percentage of adults identifying as transgender by state ranged from lows of 0.30 percent in North Dakota, 0.31 percent in Iowa and 0.32 percent in Wyoming to highs of 0.78 percent in Hawaii, 0.76 percent in California and 0.75 percent in Georgia.

In some states the results at first glance seemed surprising. In New York, for example, the percentage was 0.51; in Texas it was 0.66.

"From prior research, we know that trans people are more likely to be from racial and ethnic minorities, particularly from Latino backgrounds," Jody L. Herman, a scholar of public policy at the institute, said. "And they are also younger."

"So state demographics on race and age can impact the percentage of trans people in those states," she added.

A comparable estimate for transgender youth in the United States does not yet exist. As elusive as the adult numbers are to track, figures for adolescents, who are already in a molting process of identity, are harder still. Researchers have not yet concurred on a reliable method to tabulate transgender teenagers, much less younger children, though they are at the center of the debates over school bathroom policies.

The new figures were drawn from a question that 19 states elected to pose in 2014 as part of the Centers for Disease Control and Prevention's Behavioral Risk Factor Surveillance System, a comprehensive telephone health survey. The researchers also used Census Bureau data to develop population estimates in the remaining 31 states.

Mara Keisling, the executive director of the National Center for Transgender Equality, an advocacy and education organization based in Washington, welcomed the new estimates and predicted that in time, they would continue to rise. As she looked at the state figures, she pointed to North Carolina, currently ground zero for contested legislation about bathroom accessibility and anti-discrimination policies. Researchers estimated that state's population of transgender people to be 44,750.

"Even if it's 40,000 or 30,000, that's a lot more than they thought," Ms. Keisling said. "That helps us to say, 'Don't use us politically — you have to do something right by us. There are a lot of us living in your state.'"

Kerith Conron, a social epidemiologist at The Fenway Institute in Boston, which develops health programs for gay, lesbian, bisexual and transgender people, among others, said that the new numbers could affect planning support services more effectively.

"This shows trans elders who need gender-affirming services in nursing homes," she said. "Trans adults will need good health care. And, looking ahead, there will be more trans youth who are economically vulnerable and required to be at school."

Getting an accurate count of transgender people remains a persistent challenge for researchers. In the question posed by interviewers for the 2014 C.D.C. survey, people were asked whether they considered themselves transgender. If they replied yes, they were asked whether they considered themselves to be male-to-female, female-to-male, or gender nonconforming.

But as awareness of gender identity grows, definitions themselves are becoming even more nuanced and fluid. For example, people listed on a birth certificate as male but who as adults identify as female may not consider the term transgender to apply to them.

To capture a more complete portrait of the population, newer surveys are beginning to frame the transgender question in two steps, first asking about gender assigned at birth, and then about current gender identity.

Those results would include people who call themselves transgender, and those who identify as a gender that differs from the one on their original birth certificate.

Andrew R. Flores, a public opinion and policy fellow at the Williams Institute, said that in time, the available data would become richer still. At least five more states have added the optional transgender question to their C.D.C. telephone health surveys, he said.

Boy Scouts, Reversing Century-Old Stance, Will Allow Transgender Boys

BY NIRAJ CHOKSHI | JAN. 30, 2017

REVERSING A STANCE of more than a century, the Boy Scouts of America said on Monday that the group would begin accepting members based on the gender listed on their application, paving the way for transgender boys to join the organization.

"For more than 100 years, the Boy Scouts of America, along with schools, youth sports and other youth organizations, have ultimately deferred to the information on an individual's birth certificate to determine eligibility for our single-gender programs," the group said in a statement on its website. "However, that approach is no longer sufficient as communities and state laws are interpreting gender identity differently, and these laws vary widely from state to state."

The announcement, reported on Monday night by The Associated Press, reverses a policy that drew controversy late last year when a transgender boy in New Jersey was kicked out of the organization about a month after joining.

"After weeks of significant conversations at all levels of our organization, we realized that referring to birth certificates as the reference point is no longer sufficient," Michael Surbaugh, the Scouts' chief executive, said in a recorded statement on Monday.

The announcement came amid a national debate over transgender rights, with cities and states across the nation struggling with whether and how to regulate gender identity in the workplace, in restrooms and at schools.

In recent years, the Boy Scouts of America have expanded rights for gay people. In 2013, the group ended its ban on openly gay youths participating in its activities. Two years later, the organization ended its ban on openly gay adult leaders.

Advocates for gay and transgender people who had pushed for changes in Boy Scouts' policy praised Monday's announcement.

"From our perspective, they clearly did the right thing," said Zach Wahls, who co-founded Scouts for Equality, a nonprofit group that advocates for stronger protections in the organization for gays and transgender people. "My team and I knew that they were considering a policy change, but we are both heartened and surprised by how quickly they moved to change the situation."

The announcement came less than three months after Joe Maldonado, an 8-year-old transgender boy, was kicked out of a Cub Scout pack in Secaucus, N.J., because of his birth gender. It may have been the first such ejection in the country, Mr. Wahls said.

On Monday, Joe, who will turn 9 on Wednesday, said he was glad for the reversal.

"I think it's pretty cool that I get to go back in," he said.

His mother, Kristie Maldonado, however, said she was conflicted when representatives from the local Boy Scout chapter called on Monday to inform them of the reversal. She said she had already begun the process of filing a discrimination complaint against the chapter.

"I believe the only reason they called is because of that," she said. Still, she added, when she first heard the announcement, she felt "ecstatic, delighted."

Joe was upset by the initial decision to kick him out of the group, he told The Record, a newspaper in northern New Jersey, at the time.

"It made me mad," he said. "I had a sad face, but I wasn't crying. I'm way more angry than sad. My identity is a boy. If I was them, I would let every person in the world go in. It's right to do."

After Joe was removed from the Boy Scouts last fall, he and his mother enlisted the help of Garden State Equality, a group that advocates for lesbian, gay, bisexual and transgender rights and had worked with the Maldonados before. With that help, they were able to raise awareness about Joe's dismissal locally and then nationally.

Mr. Wahls, an Eagle Scout, said that when he helped found Scouts for Equality in 2012, the Boy Scouts of America did not yet allow gay scouts or leaders, and "there was zero conversation about transgender issues."

While he was encouraged by what appeared to be the group's quick decision on accepting transgender scouts, Scouts for Equality plans to push for a more formal policy, Mr. Wahls said.

"We want to make sure that they work with experts who have experience with transgender youth and youth programs," he said.

The Boy Scouts of America claim nearly 2.3 million members between the ages of 7 and 21, and the group counts many notable figures among its alumni and volunteers.

One of them, Rex W. Tillerson, President Trump's nominee for secretary of state, was involved in getting the organization to accept gay scouts and leaders. He was the national president of the Boy Scouts of America from 2010 to 2011 and served on the group's executive board in 2013 when it voted to lift the ban on gay scouts.

That decision came after years of reluctance from the organization and a wrenching internal debate that involved threats from some conservative parents and volunteers that they would quit. When the ban on gay leaders was reversed in 2015, the Mormon Church, the largest sponsor of scouting units, briefly threatened to leave the group as well.

She? Ze? They? What's in a Gender Pronoun

BY JESSICA BENNETT | JAN. 30, 2016

WASHINGTON — What happens when 334 linguists, lexicographers, grammarians and etymologists gather in a stuffy lecture hall on a Friday night to debate the lexical trends of the year?

They become the unlikely heroes of the new gender revolution.

That's what happened here earlier this month anyway, at a downtown Marriott, where members of the 127-year-old American Dialect Society anointed "they," the singular, gender-neutral pronoun, the 2015 Word of the Year. As in: "They and I went to the store," where they is used for a person who does not identify as male or female, or they is a filler pronoun in a situation where a person's gender identity is unknown.

"Function words don't get enough love," a man argued from the floor. (Function words, I would later learn, are words that have little lexical meaning but serve to connect other words — or "the basic building blocks in language," according to Ben Zimmer, the event's M.C.)

"We need to accept 'they,' and we need to do it now," shouted another linguist, hidden behind the crowds.

"As a gender neutral pronoun, 'they' has been useful for a long time," said Anne Curzan, an English professor at the University of Michigan. ("They" can be found in the works of literary greats like Chaucer and Jane Austen.) "But I think we've seen a lot of attention this year to people who are identifying out of the gender binary."

Gender binary: That's the idea that there are two distinct genders, one male and one female, with nothing in between.

But to Ms. Curzan's point: Indeed. If we've learned anything over the last year, from vocal transgender spokespeople like Caitlin Jenner and Laverne Cox; from on-screen depictions like "Transparent," the Emmy-winning Amazon series about a family patriarch who comes out as transgender; or even from Miley Cyrus — who has said she identifies as "pansexual," or sexually fluid — it's that both sexuality (whom you go to bed with) and gender (who you go to bed as) are much more ... flexible.

"I think we, and particularly young people, increasingly view gender not as a given, but as a choice, not as a distinction between male and female, but as a spectrum, regardless of what's 'down there,'" said Julie Mencher, a psychotherapist in Northampton, Mass., who conducts school workshops on how to support transgender students. "Many claim that gender doesn't even exist."

It does exist when it comes to language, though. He, she, hers, his, male, female — there's not much in between. And so has emerged a new vocabulary, of sorts: an attempt to solve the challenge of talking about someone who identifies as neither male nor female (and, inevitably, the linguistic confusion that comes along with it).

These days, on college campuses, stating a gender pronoun has become practically as routine as listing a major. "So it's like: 'Hi, I'm Evie. My pronouns are she/her/hers. My major is X,'" said Evie Zavidow, a junior at Barnard.

"Ze" is a pronoun of choice for the student newspaper at Wesleyan, while "E" is one of the categories offered to new students registering at Harvard.

At American University, there is "ey," one of a number of pronoun options published in a guide for students (along with information about how to ask which one to use).

There's also "hir," "xe" and "hen," which has been adopted by Sweden (a joining of the masculine han and the feminine hon); "ve," and "ne," and "per," for person, "thon," (a blend of "that" and "one"); and the honorific "Mx." (pronounced "mix") — an alternative to Ms. and Mr. that was recently added to the Oxford English Dictionary. (The "x" in Mx. is meant to represent an unknown, similar to the use of x in algebraic equations.)

Those are just the pronouns, of course.

To use them, you need to have at least some knowledge of the identities to which they correspond — beginning with an understanding of the word "identity," along with its sister verb, "identify" (as in: "I identify as female" or "I identify as mixed-race").

"Identity" was honored last month in another "word of the year" contest, this one by Dictionary.com — a choice, said Jane Solomon, a senior editor, to reflect the public's "increasing awareness" of new gender expressions (as well as an increase in lookups for their definitions).

Among the additional words and terms the dictionary was updating for the year ahead: "code-switching," or modifying of one's behavior to adapt to different sociocultural norms; "sapiosexual," for a person who finds intelligence the most sexually attractive feature; and "gender expression," or an expression of one's gender identity.

"It's like the hyper-individuation of identity," said Micah Fitzerman-Blue, a writer and producer on "Transparent," who calls himself cisgender ("cis" for short), meaning he identifies with the sex (male) he was assigned at birth (or A.A.B.). "Is there such a thing as too many pronouns? Possibly. But who am I to pick and choose? Language has a way of sorting this stuff out."

Does it, though?

In the second-to-last episode of last season's "Transparent," there was a blip of a scene that perhaps crystallized this moment in time: Ali, played by Gaby Hoffmann, stood in front of a bulletin board in the gender studies department of a university campus, waiting to speak with a professor. Tacked to the wall was a flier illustrated with a pair of boxing gloves. "Gender Pronoun Showdown!" it declared.

It was prescient.

Facebook now offers 50 different gender identity options for new users, including gender fluid (with a gender identity that is shifting), bigender (a person who identifies as having two distinct genders) and agender (a person without an identifying gender). There are day cares that proudly tout their gender-neutral pronoun policies — so kids don't feel boxed in — and college professors who are skewered on the Internet for messing them up.

In New York City, new clarifications to the city's human rights guidelines make clear that the intentional misidentification of a person's preferred name, pronoun or title is violation of the city's anti-discrimination law.

Misgendering "isn't just a style error," Caitlin Dewey of The Washington Post wrote to describe a Twitter account she created following Ms. Jenner's coming out, to "politely" correct for pronoun misuse. "It's a stubborn, longtime hurdle to transgender acceptance and equality, a fundamental refusal to afford those people even basic grammatical dignity." (The Post, Ms. Dewey's employer, recently announced the term "they" would be included in its stylebook.)

And yet the learning curve remains.

I discovered recently that "trans*," with an asterisk, is now used as an umbrella term for non-cisgender identities — simpler than listing them all (but still considered respectful). On a recent radio segment, I found out that a newer term for "cisgender" is "chromosomal," as in "chromosomal female," which denotes a person who identifies with the sex (female) she was assigned at birth. (Another way of saying that a person was "assigned female at birth" — which does not necessarily make her a "chromosomal female" — is A.F.A.B.).

As for the pronouns: "They" may or may not correspond with these identities — which is why it's in anybody's best interest to simply ask. But when you do, don't make the common mistake of calling it a preferred pronoun — as it is not considered to be "preferred."

"The language is evolving daily — even gender reassignment, people are now calling it gender confirmation!" Jill Soloway, the creator of "Transparent," said in a recent profile in The New Yorker, making the case for "they."

"It's not intuitive at all," her girlfriend, the lesbian poet Eileen Myles, said in the article.

That doesn't even begin to delve into the debate about the evolving use of "woman" and "vagina" — or, as some prefer to call it, "internal genitalia" — which is perhaps a linguistic (and political) world unto its own. Mills College recently changed its school chant from "Strong women! Proud women! All women! Mills women!" to "Strong, proud, all, Mills!"

Meanwhile, Mount Holyoke prompted a response from the iconic feminist playwright Eve Ensler after canceling a performance of "The Vagina Monologues" last year (because of its narrow view of gender). (At Columbia, that play has been replaced by a production called "Beyond Cis-terhood.")

Even the venerable NPR host Terry Gross has struggled with the language, repeatedly using the incorrect pronoun when interviewing Ms. Soloway last season about her transgender father, upon whom the show is based.

"I think there are a lot of people who want to do the right thing but are struggling to play catch-up with this new gender revolution," said Ms. Mencher, a former transgender specialist at Smith College, which is one of a handful of historically women's colleges to begin accepting transgender students.

"I begin all my trainings with an invitation for participants to stumble over language, to risk being politically incorrect, to bungle their pronouns — in the service of learning," Ms. Mencher said.

As for they: Lexicological change won't happen overnight. (Just look at the adoption of Ms.) But it does have a linguistic advantage, in that it's already part of the language.

"Whether it's the feminist movement of the 1970s or expressions of non-binary gender identities today," said Mr. Zimmer of the American Dialect Society, "social changes can help power these changes."

Milestones in the American Transgender Movement

BY THE NEW YORK TIMES | AUG. 28, 2015

Though a growing number of transgender Americans are coming out, it has been a long road. What follows is a selection of events showing the evolution of the transgender movement. Read the Transgender Today series and view the ever-expanding personal stories feature.

1952

Christine Jorgensen Becomes First American to Have a Sex Change A former Army private from the Bronx became the first American to undergo a sex change operation after traveling to Denmark for surgery and hormone treatments. Upon her return, she publicly announced her transition, and became an advocate and a celebrity.

MAY 1959

Clashes at Cooper's Donuts Police officers tried to arrest individuals at Cooper's Donuts in Los Angeles, a popular hangout for transgender people, drag queens and others in the L.G.B.T. community. The patrons clashed with the officers over the treatment, throwing coffee, doughnuts and utensils.

AUGUST 1966

Riots at Compton's Cafeteria Like Cooper's Donuts, Compton's Cafeteria in the Tenderloin District of San Francisco was one of the few places in the area where transgender people, who were not welcome at gay bars, could congregate publicly. Riots broke out there after police officers tried to kick out a transgender woman. Members of the L.G.B.T. community picketed the restaurant after it prohibited transgender people from entering.

1966

'The Transsexual Phenomenon' The physician Harry Benjamin published "The Transsexual Phenomenon," a groundbreaking book that outlined how transgender people could transition medically.

JUNE 1969

The Stonewall Riots Police officers raided the Stonewall Inn, a gay club in New York City. The crowd, weary of the raids on gay clubs, rioted. Many in the L.G.B.T. community, including transgender people, joined in several days of demonstrations. The Stonewall Riots are widely considered to have sparked the L.G.B.T. rights movement.

1970

The Street Transvestite Action Revolutionaries Sylvia Rivera and Marsha P. Johnson started Street Transvestite Action Revolutionaries, or STAR House, an advocacy group and shelter in New York.

1975

Transgender Protections in Minneapolis Minneapolis became the first city to pass a law prohibiting discrimination against transgender people.

AUGUST 1977

Renée Richards The New York Supreme Court ruled that Renée Richards, a transgender woman who played professional tennis, was eligible to play at the United States Open as a woman.

1987

In the 1987 revision of "The Diagnostic and Statistical Manual of Mental Disorders," the American Psychiatric Association added "gender identity disorder" as a classification for transgender people.

AUGUST 1992

First International Conference on Transgender Law and Employment Policy The conference in Houston was the first of six gatherings where activists, especially lawyers, from around the country met and laid the groundwork for the transgender movement. Speakers at the conference addressed legal issues related to health care, employment and military service, among other areas.

1993

First State Protections Minnesota became the first state to extend protections against discrimination to transgender people.

DECEMBER 1993

Brandon Teena Brandon Teena, a 21-year-old transgender man, was beaten, raped and murdered in Nebraska. His story was later shared in the film "Boys Don't Cry."

1994

The Gazebo Chat Room The Gazebo, a dedicated chat room for transgender people, was started on AOL by Gwendolyn Ann Smith, providing a gathering place and a resource center with a bulletin board. By the mid-1990s, Ms. Smith said, The Gazebo had tens of thousands of unique visitors a month.

1995

Transgender Lobbying Phyllis Frye, called the grandmother of the movement, and Riki Anne Wilchins held the first transgender lobbying day in Washington. Ms. Wilchins created GenderPAC, an advocacy group based in Washington.

1999

The Transgender Day of Remembrance The advocate Gwendolyn Ann Smith organized the first Transgender Day of Remembrance, to honor the memory of Rita Hester and other transgender people like her who were lost to bigotry and anti-transgender violence.

2001

Rhode Island Passes Law Rhode Island became the second state to include transgender people in a nondiscrimination law. Seventeen more states now do so.

2002

Advocates for the Transgender Community The Transgender Law Center, a civil rights organization that advocates for transgender communities, opened its first office in San Francisco.

MAY 29, 2003

First Transgender Person Officially Visits White House George W. Bush became the first president to officially welcome an openly transgender person, Petra Leilani Akwai, into the White House as part of a Yale 1968 class reunion.

Most of the big transgender advocacy organizations started up during the Bush years—the equality center, the Transgender Law Center, the Sylvia Rivera Law Project, the Transgender Legal Defense and Education Fund, and the Center of Excellence for Transgender Health.

JUNE 2004

A March of Our Own San Francisco's first Trans March took place.

2005

California Bans Insurance Discrimination Against Transgender Patients California became the first state to mandate transgender health care coverage with the Insurance Gender Nondiscrimination Act.

SEPTEMBER 2008

Diane Schroer Diane Schroer won a discrimination lawsuit against the

Library of Congress, after it rescinded a job offer as a terrorism analyst after learning that Ms. Schroer was transgender and intended to start the job as a woman. A District Court judge concluded that the Library of Congress was in violation of Title VII of the Civil Rights Act.

NOVEMBER 2008

A Transgender Mayor Stu Rasmussen was elected mayor of Silverton, Ore., becoming the first openly transgender mayor in America.

APRIL 2009

Murder of Transgender Woman Labeled a Hate Crime A jury in Colorado found Allen Andrade guilty of first-degree murder in the killing of Angie Zapata. The case was among the first in which a hate crime law was applied in a murder trial where the victim was transgender.

JUNE 2009

Chaz Bono Formerly known as Chastity, the child of Cher and Sonny Bono came out as a transgender man, Chaz.

2009

Presidential Appointees President Obama nominated the first openly transgender federal appointees. Dylan Orr began as an attorney at the Department of Labor in December, and a month later, Amanda Simpson became a senior technical adviser in the Commerce Department's Bureau of Industry and Security.

OCT. 17, 2010

First Openly Transgender Judge Phyllis R. Frye, a lawyer since 1981, was sworn in as a judge in Houston, becoming the nation's first openly transgender judge. Victoria Kolakowski was sworn in as the first transgender trial judge a few months later.

BRANDON THIBODEAUX FOR THE NEW YORK TIMES

Judge Phyllis Randolph Frye sits for a portrait in her office in Houston, TX, on Wednesday, July 22, 2015. With her swearing in in 2010, Judge Frye became the United States' first transgender judge. She is a senior partner with Frye, Oaks and Benavidez, PLLC, and devotes her practice to transgender clients.

NOVEMBER 2010

College Sports Kye Allums, who played basketball at George Washington University, came out as a transgender man. He is believed to be the first Division I college basketball player to compete publicly as a transgender person.

MAY 2011

A Memo on Transgender Employees The Office of Personnel Management issued a memo offering guidance to federal agencies on how to support transgender employees.

2012

The Girl Scouts of Colorado Take a Stand The Girl Scouts of Colorado welcomed all children who identify as girls. In a statement to CNN, the group said, "If a child identifies as a girl and the child's family presents her as a girl, Girl Scouts of Colorado welcomes her as a Girl Scout."

2012

Title VII Applies to Transgender Employees The Equal Employment Opportunity Commission ruled that Title VII of the 1964 Civil Rights Act, which made it illegal to discriminate based on sex, also protected transgender employees.

2013

A Change at the American Psychiatric Association The American Psychiatric Association updated its manual, "The Diagnostic and Statistical Manual of Mental Disorders," replacing the term "gender identity disorder" with one that was less stigmatizing, "gender dysphoria."

APRIL 2014

Transgender Studies Quarterly Duke University Press began Transgender Studies Quarterly, the first academic publication of its kind.

MAY 2014

A Medicare Exclusion Reversed The Department of Health and Human Services reversed a Medicare policy in place since 1981. Medicare must now cover sex reassignment surgery.

JUNE AND JULY 2014

Laverne Cox Laverne Cox, an actress in "Orange Is the New Black," became the first transgender person to appear on the cover of Time magazine. In July, she became the first transgender person to be nominated for an Emmy.

DECEMBER 2014

Changes at the Department of Justice The government agency took the position that Title VII of the Civil Rights Act of 1964 applied to claims of discrimination based on gender identity.

JAN. 11, 2015

'Transparent' The Amazon series "Transparent" won a Golden Globe for best television comedy or musical. The show's star, Jeffrey Tambor, took home the award for best actor in the category. The show also features Alexandra Billings, who was the first transgender actor to play a transgender character on television, when, in 2005, she was in "Romy and Michele: In the Beginning."

JAN. 20, 2015

Obama on Transgender President Obama mentioned transgender people in his State of the Union address, a presidential first. "That's why we defend free speech and advocate for political prisoners, and condemn the persecution of women, or religious minorities, or people who are lesbian, gay, bisexual or transgender," he said.

JUNE 1, 2015

Caitlyn Jenner Introduces Herself Caitlyn Jenner, formerly Bruce, an

Olympic gold medalist, author, actor and reality television star, discussed her transition to a woman in an article in Vanity Fair. In an acceptance speech for the Arthur Ashe Courage Award at the ESPY Awards in Los Angeles in July, she said she planned to use the attention to push for acceptance of transgender people across the world.

JULY 13, 2015

A Pentagon Shift The Pentagon announced plans to lift a ban on military service by transgender people by early next year. This was seen as a tacit recognition that thousands of transgender people are already in uniform.

AUG. 18, 2015

White House Hires an Openly Transgender Staff Member Raffi Freedman-Gurspan, who was a policy adviser at the National Center for Transgender Equality, will serve as an outreach and recruitment director on President Obama's staff.

The Struggle for Fairness for Transgender Workers

BY THE NEW YORK TIMES | JULY 9, 2015

SHORTLY AFTER graduating from college in Pennsylvania last year, Elaine Rita Mendus hopped on a Greyhound bus, hoping the $2,000 in her bank account would keep her afloat until the first paycheck. There was only one city in the country that seemed moderately promising for a 6-foot-3 transgender woman in the early stages of transitioning to launch a career.

"I figured, where else will I be accepted?" Ms. Mendus, 24, said. "New York."

It was a rude awakening. The luckiest break she caught after a monthslong quest to find steady work was a coveted slot at one of the city's few homeless shelters that give refuge to gay and transgender youths for a few months. It was a blessing, she said, but also "a really strange pill to swallow."

Americans' understanding of transgender people has been shaped recently by the riveting, glamorous lives of the former Olympian Caitlyn Jenner and the actress Laverne Cox. The two, though, are far from representative of an economically disadvantaged community that continues to face pervasive employment discrimination, partly as a result of lagging legal protections.

Roughly 15 percent of transgender Americans earn less than $10,000 a year, a rate of extreme poverty that is almost four times higher than the national average, according to the National Center for Transgender Equality and the National Gay and Lesbian Task Force. They are twice as likely to be unemployed as the general population, though transgender Americans have a higher level of education than the general population. About 16 percent of respondents to a 2011 survey said they resorted to illegal trades like prostitution and drug dealing. Ninety percent said they faced harassment, mistreatment or

DAMON WINTER/THE NEW YORK TIMES

Elaine Rita Mendus

discrimination on the job. The worst off are black and Hispanic transgender women, particularly those who don't have the means to alter their physical appearance as much as they would like. For many, coming out means being drawn into a cycle of debt, despair and dreadful choices.

In 1993, Minnesota became the first state to enact a law protecting employees from discrimination on the basis of gender identity. Since then, 18 other states, the District of Columbia, Puerto Rico and scores of jurisdictions have taken similar steps, which today collectively cover about 51 percent of the population.

In 2012, the Equal Employment Opportunity Commission began taking the position that discrimination against transgender employees was a form of sex discrimination under the Civil Rights Act of 1964. That offers individuals valuable legal recourse, but pursuing claims through the E.E.O.C. is time-consuming and generally futile for those who cannot afford to hire a lawyer.

Bills to protect lesbian, gay, bisexual and transgender workers from discrimination have been introduced in Congress, but none have passed. A federal law would help by prompting employers to update personnel policies and increase awareness of illegal bias. As things stand now, laws barring gender identity-based discrimination vary considerably from state to state and city to city.

"That really contributes to a lot of confusion for employers who aren't clear of what their obligations are under the law," said Sarah Warbelow, the legal director at the Human Rights Campaign. "Part of what feeds into workplace culture is a firm grasp on what legal obligations the employer has to the employee."

New York State lawmakers, for instance, passed a bill in 2002 to bar discrimination against gays and lesbians, but have not enacted a law to protect transgender workers. New York City laws bar discrimination based on sexual orientation and gender identity, but transgender people and their advocates say discrimination, often subtle, remains common in a city widely regarded as very liberal.

Stronger legal protections can make a difference. Though they won't change intolerant attitudes overnight, they have historically helped other minorities and gradually made workplaces more inclusive.

Ms. Mendus, who is of Puerto Rican descent and studied geography and Latin American studies at Indiana University of Pennsylvania, spent the first few weeks in town applying for jobs online, but got few promising leads and none in journalism, her top choice. A paid internship in the Bronx working on an H.I.V. prevention campaign sustained her from July to November, but when those checks stopped, she became desperate to find work.

She began pounding the pavement, a stack of résumés in hand, willing to do virtually anything. Applying for a bartender position, she was brusquely told, "We don't hire guys." At a Duane Reade drugstore she used her birth name on an application, even though it did not correspond with the identification form she had on hand. "The guy looked at me like I had three heads," she said.

She got the same answer everywhere: Sorry, and good luck. In November, Ms. Mendus went to a city-run employment center in Harlem to get coaching. A counselor told her she should show up at job interviews dressed as a man, using a male name. She could try to transition once she proved herself on the job, he suggested.

"It was not the most affirming thing to be told to lie and go back in the closet," she said.

Young transgender people in New York often end up sleeping on the streets or in subway cars, waiting for a bed at one of the homeless shelters for gay and transgender youths to become available. To survive, many wind up turning to the underground economy, and some, advocates say, have reportedly exposed themselves to H.I.V. in hopes of becoming eligible for housing and assistance programs that serve people with AIDS.

"One of the few areas where transgender people are in demand is sex work," said Carl Siciliano, the executive director of the Ali Forney Center, which operates a network of shelters for gay, lesbian and transgender youths. "You have the law of supply and demand. Here are all these trans people struggling to get an economic foothold and here's where the demand is."

Ms. Mendus has met several transgender sex workers and others who have found ways to live off of welfare. An older woman urged her to "claim you're crazy, get on public housing and make them take care of you." Expanding transgender legal protections would keep more skilled people in the work force and fewer from drifting into the illicit economy for survival.

While stronger protections emerge, employers can do their part by establishing clear guidance for managers and recruiters. Federal government agencies and several large companies that have done so in recent years have found that it makes good business sense. The Human Rights Campaign, which runs a corporate equality index, has had great success in encouraging large employers to adopt policies that protect and attract gay and transgender workers. In 2002, 13 major businesses qualified for a 100 percent ranking. Today, 366 do.

"I think companies recognize diversity is a core American value," said Ms. Warbelow. "Embracing diversity among employees, they're able to attract the best and the brightest."

Moving into Trinity Place Shelter, which is run out of the basement of a church on the Upper West Side, in January gave Ms. Mendus a chance to be more strategic about her job search. In April, she got a job at a vegan restaurant on the Upper West Side, and since then, she has managed to save $500 a month.

Recently, she took and passed the test to be considered for a slot in the New York Police Department academy. She's hoping to become one of the 1,300 officers the city is adding to the force. Eventually, she would like to be able to investigate sex crimes. "It's something I've really come to care about," she said.

Medicaid Work Requirements Are Yet Another Burden for Trans Workers

BY CYRÉE JARELLE JOHNSON | FEB. 5, 2018

THE OVERLAPPING ISSUES of health care and employment discrimination remain pivotal ones for transgender communities. They became more so last month, when the Trump administration decided to allow states to institute work requirements for Medicaid.

The unemployment rate for trans people is three times higher than the national average, according to a 2015 survey produced by the National Center for Transgender Equality — a rate that results, in many cases, from anti-trans job discrimination. These new rules create a double bind for the most vulnerable trans people: Find work amid rampant prejudice and mistreatment, or lose critical medical coverage.

In Kentucky, the first state to adopt work requirements, one in four transgender people report losing a job, being passed over for a promotion or not being hired because they are trans. The majority of states considering adopting work requirements are among the 30 in which gender identity is not considered a protected category. Of the 10 states currently carrying out or proposing Medicaid work requirements, only two — Maine and Utah — have an employment nondiscrimination law in place that protects trans workers. In contrast, Arkansas and North Carolina have state-level bans on local nondiscrimination ordinances that would safeguard the rights of queer and trans communities.

Statistics regarding transgender people who lose their jobs because of their gender identities reveal only the cases in which such bias was blatant. Lost within these numbers are the more ambiguous stories — of managers who may have rejected a request for a uniform that reflected an employee's gender, workers terminated for requests to change their names on internal documents or employees whose presence was shown, through the actions of colleagues and superiors, to be unwelcome.

YANA PASKOVA FOR THE NEW YORK TIMES

A protest for transgender rights in New York City in 2017.

These stories aren't quantifiable, but they are common. These statistics also fail to factor in the basic administrative challenges unique to trans workers, who can be subject to outsize scrutiny during hiring because of discrepancies in identity documents, with their names or gender markers varying from official documents. This is particularly true in Kentucky, where nearly four in five trans people do not have identity documents that match their name and gender.

Seema Verma, the administrator for the Centers for Medicare and Medicaid Services, says that new regulations are needed because the addition of able-bodied adults without children to Medicaid under the Affordable Care Act has jeopardized the program for those whose medical conditions make them unable to work.

But trans people may be legally excluded from this population as well. Being trans itself is not a disability. But many trans people have a condition called gender dysphoria, defined in the American Psychiatric Association's "Diagnostic and Statistical Manual of Mental

Disorders" as a "marked incongruence between one's experienced/expressed gender and assigned gender." This condition can be disabling: The challenges of renegotiating everyday life while in the process of transition, often while being subjected to discrimination, can be psychologically extreme. It can also be expensive: Without insurance, transition costs can run into the tens of thousands of dollars.

Yet gender dysphoria is not recognized under the current Americans with Disabilities Act, which is supposed to protect against discrimination, and although some transgender claimants have been allowed to file under existing disability law, many others have been excluded. It is unclear whether gender dysphoria will be among the disabilities to which Ms. Verma refers, an opacity that, in itself, will discourage many trans people from seeking the program's protection.

Medicaid work requirements, coupled with a lack of legal protections for those dealing with a potentially disabling condition, leaves trans people in an untenable position: In order to receive health care, those able to work must seek employment in places that offer them few protections against discrimination, while those who are unable to work face expensive medical bills and may have nowhere to turn.

Medicaid work requirements are an attempt to roll back the Affordable Care Act's expansions in medical coverage. But when employers essentially have free rein to punish trans people for being trans, such requirements be cannot be considered fair.

Ms. Verma asserts that Medicaid work requirements are "about helping people achieve the American dream." They are far more likely to dehumanize trans people and prevent Americans from accessing necessary medical care.

How Should High Schools Define Sexes for Transgender Athletes?

BY MALIKA ANDREWS | NOV. 8, 2017

INDIANAPOLIS — The calls to high school sports officials from athletic directors and administrators began several years ago and have only become more frequent and difficult: How are you handling transgender students who want to play sports?

With widespread disagreement over where the line should be drawn between sexes for purposes of athletic competition, the question has challenged the people who set rules for Olympics sports and those who govern college sports in the United States. At the high school level, the issue has been even more vexing.

"Quite frankly, I don't think anyone has it exactly right because if they did, everyone else would just do that," said Jamey Harrison, deputy director of the governing body of high school sports in Texas. "If you look at what the N.C.A.A. is doing and what the Olympics committee is doing — and those are different because they're largely dealing with adults, versus we are working with minors — it doesn't seem like anybody has landed on something that is universally applicable."

The issue has touched off debate among coaches, athletes, parents, doctors and medical ethicists. Established guidelines at the youth level that address things like hormonal treatment and sex reassignment surgery are nonexistent.

Harrison said the issue first emerged in Texas in 2012, when the state governing body — the University Interscholastic League — had rules that required female athletes to compete on girls' teams and males on boys' teams, but no rule that addressed how to decide someone's sex.

Transgender students — those who identify as a different gender than their biological sex — did not fit into an existing category.

"We had more and more schools who said, 'We have a student who is transitioning or transitioned,'" Harrison said in a phone interview.

"I think without question, it has become much more of a common issue than it had previously been. There are strong feelings on all sides and people are very passionate about their stance. It has been a challenge."

With no national governing body laying down rules, individual states have navigated the issue independently, weighing the shifting beliefs of schools, parents and athletes.

In Texas, superintendents from member schools voted in a referendum that the governing body should use birth certificates to determine a student's sex. Indiana uses anatomical sex to determine what team a student can play on. Other states, including California, have adopted rules that allow students to use bathrooms and locker rooms and participate on the teams that align with the gender the person identifies as.

The issue is particularly nettlesome with individuals who have transitioned from male to female because of the belief that they might still have a physical advantage until their hormone therapy — which not every transgender person chooses to have — is complete.

"When you start talking about transgender athletes, a male-to-female individual, we want to ensure that that is truly a decision that is permanent," said Bobby Cox, the commissioner of the Indiana High School Athletic Association. "It is not a decision that, 'I just decided today that I am going to be a girl and I am going to go play on a girls' team' and perhaps, disadvantage those kids that are on the team and imbalance the competition.

"And as we progress down this path," he added, "and as we spend more time and energy with advocacy groups and medical professionals in this area, I think that there will be additional amendments to our policies."

There is no reliable data on the number of transgender high school athletes. Only about 0.6 percent of the adult population identifies as transgender, according to federal data from 2016. Researchers from the Williams Institute, who conducted the study, reported that 0.56 percent of adults in Indiana reported identifying as transgender.

In Texas, 0.66 percent of adults said they identify as transgender, the fifth-highest percentage in the country (behind Hawaii, California, New Mexico and Georgia). Still, transgender children are considered an at-risk minority outside of sports. According to The New England Journal of Medicine, the rate of suicide attempts among transgender people is 40 percent, compared to 4.6 percent among those who are not transgender.

Relatively new policies are already being massaged and amended. In July, the Indiana state association voted unanimously to adjust its surgery requirement. It now no longer requires transgender students who are transitioning from female to male to have sex reassignment surgery in order to compete in the gender with which they identify. But that stipulation is still in place for someone transitioning from male to female.

The group asserts it is acting in the name of fairness, but transgender rights activists accuse members of simply not wanting transgender people to participate, out of fear that those athletes will have an unfair advantage.

Olivia, who asked to be identified by first name, is transgender — born with male sex organs but now identifying as female. A high school sophomore in Indiana, she kept her gender a secret from her coaches while playing freshman tennis so that she could play on the girls' team. A handful of her teammates know that she is transgender, but it had not come up as a problem. Olivia's mother, Melissa, said that she did not think the tennis coach knew that she was not biologically female.

When the state sports association did not loosen its surgery requirement for male-to-female athletes, Olivia and her family decided to fight the ruling.

"Imagine you are practicing your favorite sport one day when somebody comes and tell you that you are not able to participate on the team," Olivia wrote in a letter to association's committee members. "So many emotions are swirling through your head: confusion, anger, embarrassment. Not only does this take away your right to play, but it takes away something that defines you."

Indiana is not the only state that uses biological sex to determine what team an athlete is eligible to play on. The Nebraska School Activities Association assembles a Gender Identity Eligibility Committee composed of a physician, psychiatrist, a school administrator and an association staff member. One criterion the committee may consider when deciding whether the student's Transgender Student Application is approved is if the student has had surgery.

Dr. Dennis Fortenberry, who facilitates a clinic for transgender youth at Riley Hospital in Indianapolis, said that he is concerned that the Indiana state association's rule is "essentially a full prohibition" of transgender participation in high school sports.

"It's a practical prohibition because the complete set of surgeries — there are multiple — and completing all of them while someone has high school eligibility left is practically impossible," Fortenberry said in a phone interview. "I've never seen anyone under the age of 18 have both top and bottom surgery. That doesn't mean those individuals don't exist, but I haven't seen them."

Harrison said the Texas association did not consult medical personnel when the birth certificate rule was initially implemented in August 2016. A medical advisory subcommittee that included Texas Children's Hospital endocrinologist David Paul was formed when Senate Bill 2095 was proposed in February. The bill would have allowed the state athletics association to disqualify athletes who are taking steroids, including testosterone, if it deemed a student was getting an unfair competitive advantage. The committee met once and Dr. Paul called in to the meeting.

Dr. Paul said that if fairness is the concern, schools should be looking at students' testosterone levels. Testosterone helps build muscle mass. Before puberty, boys and girls have similarly low testosterone levels, causing them to have similar builds and physical capabilities. After puberty, a healthy adult male will have testosterone levels far above that of a healthy woman.

Dr. Paul said that if someone is taking enough testosterone to be within the post-puberty male range, even if he was born biologically female, he should be competing against males. And to have balanced competition, people who are transitioning from male to female should have to have their testosterone levels within female range in order to compete against women, he said.

"The problem is, what testosterone level confers an advantage?" Dr. Paul said. "Testosterone has been scientifically proven to increase the athletic performance and that's part of the reason adolescent boys have higher high jump records and faster 100 meter times than adolescent girls. If part of that is testosterone driven, then you can't allow a male to compete against women. It wouldn't be fair. If you are a transgender person — whether you are trans female or trans male — it really depends on how much testosterone you have."

Joanna Harper, a medical physicist, conducted a study examining the race times of transgender athletes, trying to prove whether taking hormones had an effect on their performances. Over a period of seven years, she collected transgender female runners' race times. The study found that "collectively, the eight runners had much slower race times in the female gender than as males." The study suggests that it is possible to achieve athletic fairness through hormone therapy.

Some transgender activists argue that no one should be forced to alter their body with hormones or surgery. Hormone therapy can be expensive and inconvenient.

Despite complications with individual state policies, Harrison and Cox said they had reservations about having a national institution set rules for all high school sports.

"Having a single gender policy for all state associations would be very difficult," Cox said. "I think it would be difficult because of what people believe in California is not necessarily what people believe in Iowa. Our country is diverse. State associations should make those decisions as opposed to a national body because they are more well versed in their individual state needs. That job is better left to state associations that are closer to the member school and have relationships with the member schools."

These Transgender Children Say They're Thriving. They Want to Help Others Do the Same.

BY CHRISTINA CARON | FEB. 20, 2018

CHAZZIE IS 11 years old. She has long, wavy hair and large, expressive eyes. She listens to Demi Lovato and Ariana Grande. She really likes playing Monopoly.

Chazzie was also assigned male at birth. But that, she says, isn't what's important.

"People just, like, see me as a girl," she said.

On Sunday, Chazzie and five other transgender children and teenagers from across the country hung out in an elegant prewar apartment on the Upper West Side, ahead of their Tuesday appearance on NBC's "Megyn Kelly Today."

For some, it would be their news media debut. Others have fought for transgender rights in their home states and were well acquainted with the press. But all had the same hope: to shift the conversation about transgender youth from one that dwells on bullying, suicide and murder, to one that focuses on positivity, through an online campaign called the GenderCool Project.

The organization was co-founded by Chazzie's mother, Jen Grosshandler, who left a decades-long career in public relations and marketing about 18 months ago after working for some of the biggest brands in the world.

Chazzie was born into an "uber masculine" household, Ms. Grosshandler said, with three older brothers. But from the time she was a toddler, she was drawn to toys and games traditionally associated with girls. When Chazzie was around 4 years old, she walked down the staircase with a white Hanes T-shirt wrapped on top of her head.

YANA PASKOVA FOR THE NEW YORK TIMES

Chazzie, center, watched Gia and Nicole put on makeup before heading outside to explore New York City. They are involved with the GenderCool Project, which seeks to highlight positive stories about transgender children.

Chazzie said: "Mom, Dad look at me — isn't my hair awesome? Isn't it fabulous? I want long hair," Ms. Grosshandler recalled.

Years later, Chazzie cried while getting ready for school, and asked: "Mom, what happens if I'm a girl? Because I really believe I am a girl. What will happen to me? Will you love me? Will Dad love me? Will my brothers love me?"

"That was a huge moment for us," Ms. Grosshandler said. She eventually left her consulting practice to focus on advocacy.

Soon after, she created the GenderCool Project with Gearah Goldstein, a transgender woman who trains people on how to create gender-inclusive environments.

"Our mission is to just get rid of the stigmas and just live our lives," said Nicole, one of the participants. "And that's what everybody else is doing. So my question to the world is: 'Why can't we? Why should we not?'"

MEET THE 'CHAMPIONS'

The project seeks to humanize members of a minority group who are increasingly visible but who find their gender identity at times overshadowing everything else about them.

"I think it's pretty unique," said Debi Jackson, a family organizer at the National Center for Transgender Equality. There are a lot of websites that explain how to navigate a child's transition, she said, but they aren't focused on celebrating the kid you have.

Being "gender cool" is about being "cool with whomever anyone else is," Ms. Grosshandler said. She calls the participants champions. And their stories are aspirational rather than full of adversity.

Gia, 14, is one of her school's top field hockey players and a straight-A student. Nicole, 16, is an actress with perfectly manicured nails who hopes to appear on Broadway one day. Stella, 13, lobbies politicians for protections for trans students. Landon, 15, is an accomplished trumpet player and artist whose latest work explores "how society puts down men and boys for being feminine." Daniel, 12, is a photographer. (Their last names and hometowns are being withheld to protect their privacy.)

On Sunday, they sat side by side, laughing and chatting as if they had known one another for years, even though their first meeting in person was only a day earlier. Later, a spirited game of Never Have I Ever ("Never have I ever been to Sephora!" "Never have I ever legally changed my name!") was followed by a snowball fight in Central Park. Together, they were buoyant.

"We're all diamonds. Being trans is just one face, one edge of the diamond," Landon said. "But there is so much else that makes us diamonds. It's not just a single sliver."

'I JUST WANT TO SHOW OTHER PEOPLE THAT THEY'RE NOT ALONE'

When Gia first transitioned, she was nervous. She had heard only negative stories about transgender people.

"I was confused, honestly," she said. "Should I really transition? Like, what's going to come of this?"

Once she did, her fears subsided. "I haven't had a single person make fun of me."

That wasn't everyone's experience. Stella was bullied, and Nicole said she hadn't seen her father in four years because he does not approve of her gender identity.

"But I had a very supportive family, except for him," Nicole said. "I had a very supportive school."

She and the other participants said they hoped to make the world a less lonely place.

"When other kids see this, they can be like: 'Oh my God, I'm like that. I'm like that girl,'" Chazzie said, wiping tears from her eyes. "I just want to show other people that they're not alone."

PRESENTING A DIFFERENT NARRATIVE

An estimated 150,000 people ages 13 to 17 in the United States identify as transgender, according to a January 2017 report by the Williams Institute at the U.C.L.A. School of Law, which researches law and public policy on gender identity and sexual orientation.

In December, a Williams Institute study of gender nonconforming youths in California found that they were more than twice as likely as their gender conforming peers to have experienced psychological distress. The 2015 National School Climate Survey found that transgender students experienced more hostility than others. And four out of 10 transgender adults report having attempted suicide, according to a 2017 study by Human Rights Campaign and the Trans People of Color Coalition, the majority having done so before age 25.

The outlook for transgender youth often improves, however, when they say they feel supported.

According to the group Trans Student Educational Resources, those with supportive parents were much more likely to have high self-esteem and less likely to suffer from depression.

"I see these kids thriving all the time," said Stella's mother, Lisa. "It's not newsworthy because it's not tragic or sensationalized."

It's important to highlight the difficulties faced by trans people, she said. "But it's also equally important to show how extraordinary these kids are."

A CAMPAIGN AIMED AT 'FOLKS IN EVERY TOWN'

Ms. Grosshandler and Ms. Goldstein have rolled their campaign out strategically.

They introduced it in February because at this time last year, President Trump rescinded protections for transgender students that had allowed them to use bathrooms corresponding with their gender identity.

And they appeared on "Megyn Kelly Today" because her program appeals to different groups, Ms. Grosshandler said, including "many people who have never met a young transgender child."

Ms. Kelly, a former Fox News host, wasn't necessarily an obvious choice. But "we felt so strongly that we wanted to talk to folks in every town, in every community," Ms. Grosshandler said.

The GenderCool Project is a call to action, Ms. Goldstein said. "What are you doing for the community? How are you using voices, how are you telling stories, how are you being inclusive?" As a transgender adult, she added, "I wish I had some positive messaging around when I was growing up."

Who Gets to Play the Transgender Part?

BY BROOKS BARNES | SEPT. 3, 2015

LOS ANGELES — More than at any time in its history, Hollywood is under enormous pressure to find performers who match the racial and ethnic traits of characters.

Ridley Scott was harshly criticized for using non-Egyptian actors to play Egyptians in "Exodus." The director Cameron Crowe faced an online mob for casting Emma Stone as an Asian-American woman in "Aloha." (He ultimately apologized.) When Warner Bros. announced that Rooney Mara would play Tiger Lily in its forthcoming "Pan," the studio was served with a petition headlined "Stop Casting White Actors to Play People of Color!"

But does it remain acceptable — at this Caitlyn Jenner and Laverne Cox moment — for non-transgender actors and actresses to play transgender characters?

Hollywood is about to find out. Two high-profile new films, each with Oscar aspirations, star performers who are not transgender in major transgender roles. On Saturday, "The Danish Girl," with Eddie Redmayne in the title role, will have its world premiere at the Venice Film Festival. "About Ray," starring Elle Fanning as a teenager in early gender transition, arrives next Saturday at the Toronto International Film Festival.

Both casting decisions reflect what remains the dominant view in movies and television. A dozen casting directors, producers, network programmers and studio executives said in interviews that transgender roles were best filled by finding the best actor or actress, regardless of gender identity. In other words, acting is acting. Besides, they asked, don't transgender performers want to be considered for non-transgender roles?

Peter Saraf, a producer of "About Ray," which is to be released in theaters on Sept. 18, said emphatically at the start of an interview that Hollywood needed to work "a lot harder to create opportunities for trans actors to play any kind of role." That said, he defended the casting of Ms. Fanning.

"We try to make the strongest creative choices we can," he said. "Elle, who is one of the most exciting and extraordinary actresses working today, was passionate about the role, and we had the confidence that she could carry a movie."

But some advocates believe that it is flatly offensive for a non-transgender performer to play a transgender part. Jos Truitt, executive director of development at Feministing, an online network, put it this way: When actors like Mr. Redmayne and Jared Leto (who won an Oscar for his portrayal of Rayon in "Dallas Buyers Club") play these roles, it perpetuates "the stereotype that trans women are just men in drag."

At least in some corners of Hollywood, a similar position is gaining steam.

"At this moment in time, especially, I think this industry has a responsibility to put trans actors in trans roles," said Sean Baker, who directed "Tangerine," an independent film that was released in July and starred two transgender actresses. "To not do it seems very wrong in my eyes. There is plenty of trans talent out there."

Adding complexity to the matter, Glaad, which aggressively monitors Hollywood's depictions of gay, lesbian, bisexual and transgender characters, has taken a more nuanced stance. Jeffrey Tambor plays a retired professor beginning a transition on Amazon's "Transparent," and in March that series won a Glaad Media Award, a prize that lists "fair, accurate and inclusive representations" among its criteria.

"There is a consensus that trans actors bring a certain authenticity to a trans role and that trans actors should also have the opportunity to play non-trans characters," said Nick Adams, who leads Glaad's transgender efforts. Beyond that, Mr. Adams said, there is little agreement among advocates, with some supporting Ms. Truitt's hard-line position and others allowing that "in certain circumstances, a non-trans person can play a trans character if they do their homework and learn from trans people, as Jeffrey Tambor did."

For the most part, the transgender stories that Hollywood is telling focus on early transition, perhaps because that process can be mined easily for drama, Mr. Adams noted. That focus also gives studios cover to cast non-transgender performers; Mr. Redmayne must appear as a man at the beginning of "The Danish Girl," for instance. (Glaad is pushing Hollywood to focus less on transition stories.)

Movies like "About Ray" and "The Danish Girl" also face business realities.

"I'm embarrassed to say this, because I do strongly believe that we should be casting transgender performers in these parts — it matters — but often you don't even seriously consider them, because the studio needs a name for financing or marketing reasons," said one leading casting director, speaking on the condition of anonymity because, she said, she considered the topic "radioactive."

Ms. Fanning and Mr. Redmayne were not available for interviews, according to their representatives. None of the filmmakers or studio executives behind "The Danish Girl" would discuss Mr. Redmayne's casting.

"The Danish Girl" is the more high-profile film, in part because it comes from an Academy Award-winning director, Tom Hooper ("The King's Speech"), and stars the reigning best actor; Mr. Redmayne won an Oscar in February for his portrayal of Stephen Hawking in "The Theory of Everything." Mr. Hooper approached Mr. Redmayne for "The Danish Girl" in 2011, when they were working on "Les Misérables."

Mr. Hooper recently told Screen Daily that he sensed "a certain gender fluidity" in Mr. Redmayne. "The Danish Girl," set for release in theaters on Nov. 27 by the Universal-owned Focus Features, tells the true story of a Copenhagen artist who underwent sex reassignment surgery in 1930. It was one of the first such efforts.

The director Cameron Crowe faced an online mob for casting Emma Stone as an Asian-American woman in "Aloha."

In the time it took for "The Danish Girl" to be made, however, transgender issues have leaped to the cultural forefront.

Ms. Cox, the transgender actress who plays Sophia Burset on "Orange Is the New Black," appeared on the cover of Time last year. President Obama in January turned heads by using the word "transgender" in his State of the Union address. "Transparent" won best comedy series in front of 19 million viewers at the last Golden Globe Awards.

And then came Ms. Jenner, who spoke about her transition in a prime-time ABC News special, subsequently posing for the cover of Vanity Fair.

At the same time, pushback on casting decisions large and small has become harder for Hollywood to ignore. Just a few years ago, protests of insensitivity — over the hiring of Johnny Depp to play Tonto in "The Lone Ranger," for instance, or giving Jake Gyllenhaal the lead in "Prince of Persia: The Sands of Time" — were barely blips on the movie industry's radar. But fans, advocacy groups and rank-and-file critics have grown more sophisticated in their use of social media to organize and voice disappointment.

In today's Internet culture, the tendency is to shoot first and ask questions later. Nuance doesn't always matter. Tiger Lily, who exists in the public imagination (and not in a particularly sensitive way) as a Native American woman, was rewritten to be of a nonspecific race, Ms. Mara ultimately explained. "Pan" is scheduled for release on Oct. 9.

Perhaps to get ahead of any blowback, Focus recently had Mr. Redmayne explain to Out magazine how he met with many transgender women to educate himself. "Gosh, it's delicate," he said in that interview. "And complicated."

Part of the frustration with Hollywood among transgender people involves the lack of transgender characters, even with heightened cultural attention. Of the 161 mainstream and art house films that Glaad tracked in its last Studio Responsibility Index, released in April, none had a transgender character. "The list of mainstream films that have depicted transgender people as multifaceted or even recognizable human beings remains tragically short," Glaad wrote in the report.

Television, which moves faster as a business and does not face the same pressure to cast stars, is doing a better job. "Transparent," "Orange Is the New Black" and "Sense8" — notably all from streaming services — prominently feature transgender characters and transgender actors and actresses. Glaad gives particular credit to "The Fosters," an ABC Family series that features the transgender actor Tom Phelan as a transgender teenager.

Glaad is to release a report in November that assesses the television landscape from a transgender perspective. On Thursday, it released its annual Network Responsibility Index, which focuses on "the quantity and quality" of images of gay, lesbian, bisexual and transgender people on television, and used the platform to push for more transgender representation. It told CW, for instance, that it hopes to "see a transgender character make an appearance very soon."

For transgender actors and actresses, that is encouraging — if networks seek them out for any resulting roles.

"Because I am a trans woman in 2015, there are opportunities that wouldn't have existed for me three years ago," said Hari Nef, who will join the cast of "Transparent" when it returns in December. "But Hollywood still seems very wary. There is not a rush of casting agents headed our way. Let's hope that changes. I'm right here!"

Beyond Caitlyn Jenner Lies a Long Struggle by Transgender People

BY CLYDE HABERMAN | JUNE 14, 2015

BY NOW, most Americans are probably familiar with the rights movement known by the initials L.G.B.T., but they may have a better sense of the L.G.B. part — lesbian, gay, bisexual. The T, for transgender, has eluded many people. That, however, may be quickly changing with a string of developments in recent years, not the least being the emergence this month of Caitlyn Jenner, a transgender woman who was a public figure for four decades as Bruce Jenner, Olympic decathlon champion and reality-show personality.

"Bruce always had to tell a lie," she said in a video accompanying her appearance on the cover of Vanity Fair, but "Caitlyn doesn't have any secrets."

The Jenner story is a jumping-off point for the latest installment of Retro Report, a series of video documentaries examining major stories of the past and their enduring effects. The video, though, goes much farther back, to the 1960s and gay rights protests in San Francisco and New York. Transgender men and women, people whose sense of identity did not match the body they entered life with, played significant roles. But over the years they bore burdens unique to them, in part because they were unfamiliar to most Americans.

Though the statistics may not be fully reliable, their numbers in this country are commonly estimated at 700,000, or about three-tenths of 1 percent of the adult population. A survey of 4,509 Americans adults conducted in late 2013 by the Public Religion Research Institute found that 65 percent had close friends or relatives who were gay or lesbian. Transgender? Only 9 percent. Even so, awareness of transgender people and their issues is clearly growing, and not just because of Ms. Jenner.

Chaz Bono, the child of the entertainers Sonny and Cher; Chelsea Manning, the imprisoned leaker of Army secrets; Laverne Cox, the star of the Netflix drama "Orange Is the New Black"; writers like Jennifer Finney Boylan and Janet Mock — all are transgender men and women who are shaping the national discussion. "Transparent," an award-winning Amazon online video series, is about a family whose father is a transgender woman. Another show with a dad who is a transgender woman, "Becoming Us," began last week on the ABC Family network. On June 4, Barnard College in New York announced that it would join women's colleges like Wellesley, Mount Holyoke and Smith in enrolling transgender women.

Those sorts of developments suggest that transgender men and women have made strides toward acceptance. "We don't want anything other than our humanity," Ms. Boylan, who teaches at Barnard and is a contributing opinion writer for The New York Times, told Retro Report.

Yet hatred, discrimination and violence remain the daily lot for thousands. Seven transgender women, nearly all African-Americans, were murdered in the span of a month early this year. Suicides are common, including among teenagers, who become overwhelmed by the intolerance they face while dealing with their gender identities. In San Diego, Kyler Prescott ended his life last month at 14. In December, Leelah Alcorn, a 17-year-old in Ohio, threw herself in front of a moving tractor-trailer.

Other examples abound, and teenagers are hardly alone in struggling. A 2011 report by the National Transgender Discrimination Survey showed that an astounding 41 percent of the 6,450 people interviewed had tried to kill themselves — not just thought about it, but actually made the attempt.

The findings of the survey, titled "Injustice at Every Turn," cannot be generalized to all transgender and "gender nonconforming" people because the study was not based on a random sample. But people in the study who identified themselves as part of either of these groups said they had frequently experienced physical assaults. Transgender adults and teens who participated in the study said they were harassed in schools and on the street, sometimes by the police.

Some transgender activists feel shunted aside even by their brothers and sisters in the L.G.B.T. movement. "Trans people continue to be marginalized within the L.G.B.T. rights struggle, treated as tokens when convenient," Meredith Talusan, a transgender woman, wrote last June in The American Prospect magazine.

Life in prisons or in homeless shelters, never pleasant for anyone, can be a nightmare of rape and other abuses for transgender men and women. Lourdes Ashley Hunter, executive director of the Trans Women of Color Collective, left Detroit in 2002 to put down roots in New York. Homeless on her arrival and turned away by a women's shelter that would not accept her gender identity, she had no choice but to go to a men's shelter. There, she told Retro Report, she was raped in the shower by a man holding a razor blade.

"There was nothing that I can do," she recalled. When she reported the assault to shelter staff members, "they blamed me." And that, she said with tears welling, "is just a snapshot of what we have to go through just to live."

One goal of advocacy groups is to take control of their own narrative. "Language is power," Ms. Boylan said, echoing an understanding among political groups that a national debate on, say, a topic like the estate tax is shaped mightily by whether one calls it "a death tax" or "a Paris Hilton tax." The rights group Glaad, formed in the 1980s as the Gay and Lesbian Alliance Against Defamation, has issued a guide for news organizations filled with explanations about which words are acceptable and which are not. "Transgender," this advisory makes clear, is an umbrella term that can encompass various forms of identity. It may be applied to those who alter their bodies with hormones or through surgery and to those who make no physical changes.

As the guide also notes, the American Psychiatric Association in 2013 discarded the negative word "disorder" to describe transgender people. "Gender dysphoria" replaced a diagnosis that used to be called "gender identity disorder." The extent to which other phrases will seep into the mainstream remains to be seen. Take a word like "cisgender" — "cis" being a Latin prefix that means "on the same side as" — to describe people who are not transgender. The guide acknowledges that the term is "not commonly known outside the L.G.B.T. community."

The real point is "for people to get to know us," Nick Adams, who represents Glaad on transgender issues, told Retro Report. "And get to know that we're people just like everyone else."

Seventeen Transgender Killings Contrast with Growing Visibility

BY KATIE ROGERS | AUG. 20, 2015

THE BRUTAL DEATH of a 36-year-old transgender woman in Kansas City, Mo., is the latest in what activists are calling an alarming rise in anti-transgender violence.

Tamara Dominguez, who was reported to have migrated from Mexico to escape discrimination, was hit by a vehicle early Saturday and run over several times, making her the 17th transgender person reported killed this year, according to data compiled by the National Coalition of Anti-Violence Programs.

Most of the victims have been black or Hispanic.

By comparison, 12 killings of transgender people were recorded by the coalition in 2014, said Sue Yacka, a spokeswoman.

Transgender activists believe the killing in Kansas City was motivated by Ms. Dominguez's gender identity. Randall Jenson, a representative for the Kansas City Anti-Violence Project who has been working with Ms. Dominguez's family, characterized her death as an "intentional act" meant to send a message.

And those are just the killings that are reported, said Kris Hayashi, executive director of the Transgender Law Center. Mr. Hayashi said that recent media coverage had brought increased visibility to each victim, but that the killings reflected an "ongoing" state of crisis for the community.

Activists say transgender women of color, who are often poor, are most at risk of violence.

Hoping to increase visibility for the killings, transgender activists and allies are sharing pictures of victims as their deaths are reported.

Also alarming to advocates is that several of the 17 people killed have been slain just this summer. Other recent cases include India Clarke, a 25-year-old black transgender woman who was found dead in

July from a gunshot in Tampa Bay, Fla.; Kenton Haggard, a 66-year-old who activists say was transgender, and who was killed in a stabbing in July in Fresno, Calif., that was caught on video; and Kandis Capri, a 35-year-old transgender woman, who was shot and killed in Phoenix on Aug. 11.

Laverne Cox, the transgender actress, said in a statement on Thursday that a lack of national outrage over the killings "adds insult to injury."

She said transgender women of color exist at the "intersection of multiple forms of violence which are also about race, misogyny, poverty and a system that reinforces the fallacy that we shouldn't exist and don't exist."

A suspect was arrested and charged with Ms. Clarke's killing after the police found DNA evidence and a condom that contained fluid in her car. There have been no arrests in Ms. Capri's death, according to ABC 15 in Phoenix, but her family is seeking a hate crime investigation. And authorities say there is no update in Kenton Haggard's case.

Mr. Hayashi said that transgender people faced a system of discrimination — which includes lack of access to health care, education, housing and job resources — that can result in people who put themselves in "really vulnerable positions as far as the violence that we're seeing."

The organization receives about 2,500 calls a year from transgender people and their families seeking assistance, Mr. Hayashi said. The demand often outweighs the resources.

Mr. Jenson, of the Kansas City Anti-Violence Project, said that lengthy police investigations, sometimes carried out in a way that activists feel lack dignity and thoroughness, had sometimes led to tension between officers and the communities they serve.

"We get told by agencies that we're hindering the process or hurting our communities because they don't understand hate crimes or how it could work," Mr. Jenson said. "It's not a community's job to have to educate themselves on such a nuanced system and hate crime laws that do not actually work."

Tension has also occurred over how the gender of a person who either publicly or privately identifies as transgender is reflected in a police report: In Tampa, Kansas City and Fresno, the police referred to Ms. Clarke, Ms. Dominguez and Kenton Haggard by their legal — male — names, which offends activists. And questions have been raised, particularly in the case of Kenton Haggard, over whether the victim publicly identified as transgender at all, though activists include the killing in the summer's count of fatalities.

Lt. Joe Gomez, the public information officer for the Fresno police, said gender was not a factor in efforts to investigate the death. On Thursday, he said that criticism of the police had been "blown out of proportion."

"It's just not an issue in this case," he said. "We are hoping the community comes forward with more information on the suspect."

Activists Say Police Abuse of Transgender People Persists Despite Reforms

BY NOAH REMNICK | SEPT. 6, 2015

NEW YEAR'S REVELERS clamored outside the window of Shagasyia Diamond's apartment in the Bronx the day she was arrested.

Newly into 2014, she was in the midst of a dispute with her husband when officers showed up at her front door, placed her in handcuffs and escorted her to a nearby precinct. It was there, Ms. Diamond recalled, that the violations began.

Although the New York Police Department amended its patrol guide in 2012 to require respectful treatment of transgender people, Ms. Diamond, who is a transgender woman, said she was subjected to a strip search by a male officer. Two other officers watched from a few feet away, gawking as she spread her legs. Officers then placed Ms. Diamond in a cell for men, she said, where she cowered in the corner as other inmates heckled her and used the exposed toilet in her presence. When she expressed her discomfort to an officer, he replied, "You know you like it in there with all the men."

Officers snickered at Ms. Diamond throughout the process, she said, calling her a "he-she," "tranny" and "it."

"I felt totally voiceless," Ms. Diamond, who is 37 and now divorced, said recently through tears. "Like I wasn't even human. Like my safety didn't even matter."

When the patrol guide reforms were issued, advocates for transgender people lauded the changes as groundbreaking, if overdue. Officers now were required, among other provisions, to refer to people by their preferred names and gender pronouns, to allow people to be searched by an officer of their requested gender, and to refrain from "discourteous or disrespectful remarks" regarding sexual orientation or gender identity.

TODD HEISLER/THE NEW YORK TIMES

Shagasyia Diamond, 37, who is transgender, was arrested in 2014 during a domestic dispute in the Bronx. She said she was put in a cell with men and was subjected to slurs by police officers.

But in interviews with more than 20 transgender and gender nonconforming New Yorkers who have been arrested or had other contact with the police, as well as activists and lawyers representing them, they charge that three years since the regulations were adopted, police officers regularly flout them. Even as transgender visibility surges in the news media and in popular culture, and government agencies develop more sensitive policies, many transgender people continue to report that they are mocked in the most degrading terms by officers, searched roughly and inappropriately and placed in holding cells that do not correspond with their gender identity, all violations of the reforms enacted to address those very indignities.

"We're hearing the same sorts of things today that we heard five years ago," said Sharon Stapel, the executive director of the New York City Anti-Violence Project, an advocacy group for lesbian, gay, bisexual and transgender people. "Trans people are still targeted and harassed by the police for being trans."

Some activists and elected officials are calling on the Police Department's inspector general to audit the department's adherence to the reforms. At a meeting in late July with Commissioner William J. Bratton, members of the commissioner's L.G.B.T. Advisory Panel, made up of leaders in the lesbian, gay, bisexual and transgender community, also asked for an audit. Mr. Bratton showed reluctance, according to people present at the meeting, but eventually referred the group to the department's quality assurance division.

"It's one thing to make a reform on paper, but it takes a greater commitment of resources to make the necessary cultural changes," said Councilman Ritchie Torres, a Bronx Democrat who is formally requesting an audit.

"The N.Y.P.D. is a deeply intransigent, conservative institution," Mr. Torres added. "It's going to take extensive retraining for officers to fully live up to the spirit and letter of the 2012 changes."

Detective Tim Duffy, the department's liaison to the lesbian, gay, bisexual and transgender community, said the department had begun a variety of programs to address the concerns. Among other measures, he said, newly promoted sergeants, lieutenants and captains now undergo two hours of training meant to guard against profiling and other forms of mistreatment. The training familiarizes officers, for example, with police forms that now have space for a preferred name and preferred gender pronouns. He noted that in the past several years, two police officers and one school safety officer underwent gender transitions.

Although Detective Duffy said the department has had "no reports of any issues with officers not following the guidelines," he acknowledged some resistance. "Just like any big group, everybody may not agree with the policy," he said, "but we have to do our jobs."

The reforms followed years of complaints about police mistreatment, including one from 2010 in which a transgender woman who was arrested on suspicion of prostitution said an officer stomped on her head three times, breaking a tooth and a bone near her eye. Her skirt rode up, exposing her genitals, which she said the officer then twisted and squeezed. She filed a lawsuit against the city, which was settled for around $80,000.

But in 2013, a year after the guidelines were changed, Crystal Sheridan, a transgender woman arrested on suspicion of prostitution, was called a "whore" and a "man" by police officers, she said, as they took her to a Queens precinct, where she remained for several days.

"It was like I was being bullied for no reason," recalled Ms. Sheridan, 30, who said the charges were dropped by a judge.

Often rejected by their families and stymied in their pursuit of jobs, transgender people — particularly women who are members of racial minorities — experience high rates of poverty, homelessness and violent crime. They also sometimes resort to illegal activity as a means of survival. Ms. Diamond, who was arrested in the Bronx, spent 10 years in prison for robbing a gas station, she said, to get money for sex-reassignment surgery after her family in Flint, Mich., turned their backs on her.

Such circumstances, activists said, have contributed to a form of profiling. Just as African-Americans complain of being stopped for "driving while black," transgender people claim they are singled out by the police for "walking while trans," activists say.

At a transgender forum this July in the Bronx, the roughly 200 people in attendance were asked, Have you ever felt profiled or mocked by the police? Nearly every hand shot up. Have you ever complained? Nearly every hand came down.

Tasha Hodges, a 33-year-old transgender woman from East New York, Brooklyn, kept her grievances to herself after officers referred to her by a bevy of insulting titles, she said, after a 2013 arrest for trespassing. "I've learned to accept the disrespect," Ms. Hodges explained.

Mina Malik, the executive director of the city's Civilian Complaint Review Board, which investigates complaints against the police, said the organization had collected grievances from transgender people since the reforms were instituted, but that she could not provide any data.

"The C.C.R.B. is only as effective as its reputation in the community allows it to be," said Andrea Ritchie, a lawyer with the nonprofit group Streetwise and Safe. "People's experience with the C.C.R.B. is that they don't feel heard."

Ms. Malik said the review board has "historically not had the best reputation" among transgender people, which she said explained in part why "underreporting is a chronic problem" in that community. "We are working to improve it," Ms. Malik added.

Some transgender defendants have gotten redress by calling Ms. Ritchie. She said clients had phoned her from jail in anguish after being placed in cells for a different gender. Ms. Ritchie has then had to explain the new regulations to the officers in charge, often referring them to the exact page in their guides.

Detective Duffy said that officers faced a natural learning curve. "Just like the general public is learning about the trans community and learning about trans people by people coming out like Chaz Bono and Caitlyn Jenner, so are we," he said.

After her experience in the Bronx stationhouse, Ms. Diamond slipped into an intense depression, she said, during which she lost 60 pounds. Even though the district attorney dropped the charges against her, she said she still has not filed a complaint against the police, out of fear and doubt that she would not be taken seriously.

"People used to tell me things were different in New York," said Ms. Diamond, a singer who left home in 2009. "But I know better now."

Poor, Transgender and Dressed for Arrest

BY GINIA BELLAFANTE | SEPT. 30, 2016

MEASURED IN TERMS of cultural attention, it can seem like a very enlightened time to be living with an unconventional gender identity. The rights of transgender people have been a concern of presidential politics; "Transparent," the comedy about a middle-aged male political scientist in the process of becoming female, is popular and in its third season; gender-neutral bathrooms are on the rise, and opposition to them puts challengers in the position of seeming benighted and cranky, as though they hankered for a world still dominated by three television networks.

And yet, at 6:30 a.m. on Feb. 3, as she was walking toward a bus stop in the Bushwick section of Brooklyn, Natasha Martin, who is 38 and African-American, and had been thrown out of her mother's home in Virginia as a teenager for preferring to wear girls' clothes when she was a boy, did not encounter this new collective awakening. She had just lit a cigarette when a white police van pulled up and the officers inside asked her who she was, whether Natasha Martin was her real name and if she was aware that the area where she was standing was known for prostitution.

Ms. Martin joked at the time that she hadn't seen any signs, she recalled one recent afternoon. "I said: 'Who am I supposed to be prostituting to? There is no one here!'" At that point she was taken into custody, under a 40-year-old statute in the state's penal code — 240.37 — that allows the police broad discretion in arresting anyone they deem to be loitering for the purpose of engaging in prostitution.

How can this purpose be discerned? The law is vague enough to make almost any posture vulnerable to suspicion. You could be arrested while talking to two men on a corner; while talking to someone through a car window; while walking down the street with a bottle of Korbel; for going to your job selling sofas; if it happens that you have worked as a prostitute before; just for wearing something an officer decides is too provocative.

On the morning of her arrest, Ms. Martin had set out from a friend's apartment wearing a Lane Bryant tracksuit. The charges against her were eventually dropped but not before she was made to appear in court five times.

Over the past several years, the Legal Aid Society of New York has handled so many of these cases of wrongful arrest, particularly among transgender women who are black and Hispanic, that on Friday it filed a federal civil rights suit in the Southern District of New York on behalf of several plaintiffs — Ms. Martin is one of them — challenging the constitutionality of the law. Between 2012 and 2015, the Legal Aid Society says, nearly 1,300 people were arrested in New York City under the loitering law. More than 600 were convicted, and close to 240 served some time in jail. During that period, five precincts in the city were responsible for more than two-thirds of the arrests, each of the precincts serving neighborhoods that are predominantly black and Hispanic, in the Bronx and central Brooklyn.

The deployment of Statute 240.37 is, in essence, a perverse equalizer, extending the indignities of stop-and-frisk policing, experienced by so many young black and Hispanic men, to an entire population of women already facing myriad forms of discrimination. In one instance, the suit notes, over the course of two hours on a June evening last year, officers near Monroe College in the Fordham section of the Bronx arrested at least eight transgender women. The women told their lawyers that one of the officers said they were conducting a sweep to let "girls like them" and their friends know that if they were seen hanging around after midnight they would be hauled off.

The Police Department declined to comment on the suit until it was filed.

Some of the neighborhoods where transgender women are being arrested with some regularity — Bushwick, for example, and Hunts Point in the Bronx — are undergoing rapid gentrification, leading to the obvious supposition that the greater mission is to instill enough fear in the women to make them leave, and congregate somewhere else. Ms. Martin had been arrested 14 other times under the loitering statute in the early 2000s, she told me, in most instances while she had been in the meatpacking district, as it was evolving from a place of bohemian and transgressive club life to a world of croque-monsieur and Stella McCartney.

The policing of female sexuality is something bourgeois women talk about often, with little understanding that what exists largely in the realm of metaphor for them remains, for poor women, a very literal and criminalizing surveillance of how they present themselves when they leave the house. Again and again, the Legal Aid Society has represented women arrested while wearing short dresses or high heels or tight pants and, in one bizarre instance, that well-known symbol of sexual seduction: a black pea coat. Just as it is unthinkable that the same strictures would apply to a black man drinking a tallboy on a sidewalk in East New York and a private equity investor having a glass of pinot noir on his stoop on East 93rd Street, it is inconceivable that a woman in Chelsea would be stopped by the police on her way to Barry's Bootcamp in cropped leggings and a sports bra.

The loitering law that has caused so much of this unnecessary contact with the legal system was developed in the 1970s, at a time when vice was rampant in New York City. Over the years, laws almost identical to 240.37 have been found unconstitutional in six other states, including Florida. The continued application of others suggests that certain styles of policing, far from ensuring law and order, merely articulate the ways in which law enforcement seems to function in a vanished world. As police departments across the country try to incorporate more sensitivity and difference awareness training into their curriculums, to heal the ruptures and divisions that have seemed so systemic, they might include a few tutorials on how modern women dress, and what clothes tell us about one another, and don't. Let the reform begin with a subscription to Vogue.

Violence Against Transgender People Is on the Rise, Advocates Say

BY MAGGIE ASTOR | NOV. 9, 2017

ON OCT. 21, a body was found off a county road west of Corpus Christi, Tex., with bullet wounds to the chest, abdomen and shoulders.

The victim was Stephanie Montez, a transgender woman. But because the police misidentified her as a man, it was not until last week that Ms. Montez, 47, was known to be among the more than two dozen transgender Americans killed this year.

Even as transgender people have scored political victories and turned public opinion in favor of more protections, violence has risen, especially against black and Hispanic transgender women. And Ms. Montez's case shows the difficulties advocates face in tracking killings and other hate crimes.

The full death toll is impossible to determine, but by rights groups' estimates, each of the past three years has become the deadliest on record.

The Human Rights Campaign has documented the killings of 25 transgender people in the United States so far in 2017, compared with 23 last year and 21 in 2015. Other organizations, like Glaad and the Transgender Law Center, have slightly different tallies, but the trend holds.

Transgender people have been killed this year in Chicago and in Waxahachie, Tex.; in the Ozarks of Missouri and on the sidewalks of Manhattan. They have been shot, stabbed, burned and, in at least one case, pushed into a river. On average, one to two have been killed somewhere in the United States every week.

And experts say these numbers almost certainly understate the problem. Local officials are not required to report such killings to any central database, and because the police sometimes release incorrect names or genders, it can be difficult to know that a homicide victim was transgender. So advocacy groups are left to comb news reports and talk to victims' friends or family.

Even so, Sarah McBride, a spokeswoman for the Human Rights Campaign, said the rough numbers strongly indicate that violence against transgender people is increasing.

Beverly Tillery, the executive director of the New York City Anti-Violence Project, said that since the 2016 presidential election, her organization had recorded "a spike in incidents of hate violence" — both homicides and other crimes — against transgender people as well as members of the broader gay, lesbian, bisexual and transgender community.

"There is an increased climate of hate that is, in some cases, being allowed to grow," Ms. Tillery said.

Advocates say the violence is inseparable from the social climate: that anti-transgender violence and anti-transgender laws — like so-called bathroom bills, which aim to police who may use gender-specific public facilities — are outgrowths of the same prejudice.

Sixteen states have considered bathroom bills this year (though none have passed), and six have considered legislation to invalidate local anti-discrimination protections, according to the National Conference of State Legislatures. Advocates also point to actions by the Trump administration, including the rescinding of federal protections for transgender students, an effort to bar transgender troops and a Justice Department decision to stop applying workplace discrimination protections to transgender people. Yet the administration did help with the successful prosecution of a man accused of killing Kedarie Johnson, a gender-fluid Iowa teenager.

"The same stigma and the same sort of fear that is trying to be embedded in our society are the driving factors of the extreme forms of violence that are taking place," said Isa Noyola, deputy director of the Transgender Law Center. "A lot of these cases are happening in regions where there are a lack of protections and there's a lack of understanding and infrastructure for trans folks to live their daily lives."

In some sense, experts said, the increased awareness that leads to more acceptance also draws the attention of would-be perpetrators.

"There's no question that transgender people and the trans community have seen an increase in our profile and in our visibility," Ms. McBride said. "In many cases, that is a good thing. It results in more hearts and minds opening. It allows for progress legally, socially." But it may also stir up violent opposition, she said.

Almost all the murder victims in the past several years have been nonwhite women. According to the National Center for Health Statistics, the annual murder rate for Americans ages 15 to 34 is about one in 12,000. But an investigation by the news organization Mic found that for black transgender women in the same age group, the rate was one in 2,600.

"We know that when transphobia mixes with misogyny and racism, it can often have fatal consequences," Ms. McBride said.

Yet Ms. Noyola also said the brutality had brought the community together in a powerful way.

"That resilience and that power and that wisdom," she said, "is also a part of the story."

CHAPTER 2

Transgender Access Laws in Schools

One of the primary battlegrounds in the fight for transgender rights has been the halls of schools. As more and more children have transitioned publicly, schools have scrambled to create spaces that are safe for them while facing intense pressure from religious and family groups. In 2016, Obama issued a directive ordering public schools to allow students to use bathrooms corresponding to their gender identity. Leading up to and following Obama's order, students, schools and politicians struggled to understand and address these issues.

As Transgender Students Make Gains, Schools Hesitate at Bathrooms

BY JULIE BOSMAN AND MOTOKO RICH | NOV. 3, 2015

CHICAGO — Asked to call a transgender boy by a male name he has chosen for himself, teachers and administrators around the country have leaned toward a simple response: Sure. Allow a high school student who was born male but identifies as female to join the volleyball team? Fine.

But as transgender students assert themselves more, schools have hesitated at the locker room and the bathroom. Many have developed policies that require transgender students to use private changing and showering facilities, drawing opposition from these students, their parents and advocates who say the rules are discriminatory.

The Education Department on Monday gave school officials at a suburban Chicago high school 30 days to resolve a dispute with a transgender student who identifies as a girl and has sought to change and shower in the girls' locker room without restrictions; otherwise, the school risks forfeiting Title IX funding. The confrontation was an echo of battles nationwide, where the locker room and often the restroom are the stage for a fierce fight over how extensively transgender students should be accommodated.

"I think it's an issue that people are thinking about a lot," said Thad Ballard, the president of the Elko County school board in northeast Nevada, which voted in September to keep transgender students out of bathrooms and locker rooms that correspond with their gender identity. He said the move was intended to preserve "the centuries-long tradition of respecting the difference in the sexes."

"When has it ever been appropriate for a biological boy or a biological girl to be in the opposite restroom of their gender?" Mr. Ballard said. "We're all trying to think of the best way to protect the rights of all of our students, whether they're transgender or not."

California, Washington, Colorado, Connecticut, Massachusetts, New York and the District of Columbia have already adopted policies requiring schools to permit transgender students to use bathrooms and locker rooms based on the student's gender identity. In Maine, the State Supreme Court ruled last year that under the state's antidiscrimination law, a transgender girl could use the bathrooms and locker rooms for the gender with which she identified.

Eleven other states have general antidiscrimination policies on the books that might also protect the rights of transgender students in schools, said Michael D. Silverman, executive director of the Transgender Legal Defense and Education Fund.

But some state legislatures are trying to move in the opposite direction. Republican lawmakers in Wisconsin have proposed a bill that would bar transgender students from using bathrooms that correspond with their gender identity, a measure that Democrats say is discriminatory. In Minnesota in April, the State Senate, dominated by Democrats, defeated a similar measure.

In Houston on Tuesday, voters defeated a proposal that would have established nondiscrimination protections for gay and transgender residents. Supporters said the ordinance would have offered increased protections for gay and transgender people, as well as protections against discrimination based on sex, race, age and religion. Opponents said the proposal infringed on their religious beliefs, zeroing in on the protections it would have given for gender identity, particularly transgender Houstonians who were born male but identify as women.

Some school districts have faced threats of legal action and federal intervention if they exclude transgender students from the bathroom that corresponds to their gender identity.

In Arcadia, Calif., the school district entered a settlement agreement with the Department of Justice and the Education Department's Office of Civil Rights after a transgender student who identifies as male brought a complaint about being forced to sleep in a separate camp cabin during a middle school science outing. District officials worked with federal officials to create a new policy that allows transgender students access to all sex-segregated facilities based on the gender with which they identify.

David Vannasdall, superintendent of Arcadia, a school district with fewer than 10,000 students not far from downtown Los Angeles, said that in assigning the student to a separate cabin, the district had followed the advice of a lawyer who was anticipating the reactions of other parents rather than simply working with the family of the transgender student. "The problem is you have people making decisions from the basis of fear and the extremes, and that's never good for kids," Mr. Vannasdall said.

In California, the State Legislature passed a law two years ago permitting transgender students to participate in sex-segregated activities and use facilities that were consistent with their gender identity in all schools. But opponents are mounting a plan to put an initiative on the California ballot next fall that would direct all students to use facilities that correspond with the gender on their birth certificates.

"I am not questioning their sincerity," said Karen England, spokeswoman for Privacy for All, a group that is promoting the ballot initiative in California. "But the reality of their biology is that their plumbing is quite different, and I have a right to privacy, and I have the right for my daughters and granddaughters to have the right to be in a bathroom or a locker room without being exposed to the opposite gender."

Jeff Johnston, an analyst at Focus on the Family, the conservative group based in Colorado, said in an email that "girls should not have to risk being exposed to boys in locker rooms, changing rooms and restrooms."

School officials say that in cases where parents or students raise concerns, they can work through them. In San Francisco, for example, a group of Muslim students sought permission last year to pray during break times and perform ritual cleansings in the bathrooms. But some of them were concerned that if a transgender student entered the bathroom at the same time, it would be inappropriate for the girls to share space with a biological male.

"We talked about how this was a democracy and students have the right to go to the bathroom," said Kevin R. Gogin, director of safety and wellness school health programs at the San Francisco Unified School District. After discussions with the religious students, he said, they agreed that they could seek privacy by using the private stalls for their cleansing rituals.

In Los Angeles, where the district has had a policy allowing transgender students to use bathrooms and locker rooms according to their gender identity since 2004, Judy Chiasson, coordinator in the Human Relations, Diversity and Equity Department for the Los Angeles Unified School District, said that schools have had few complaints.

"All of our students tend to be pretty modest," Ms. Chiasson said. She added that unlike students in previous generations, even after physical education classes or athletic practices, students today do not tend to undress or shower in public facilities, and in bathrooms, students can use private stalls. Because of this, she said, in many cases, students do not even know whether another student is transgender or not.

A transgender student does not want "to invade anybody else's privacy," Ms. Chiasson said. "She's in the bathroom to do her business."

The school district in Palatine, Ill., that was reproached by the Education Department this week had required a transgender student to change her clothes and shower separately from other students, causing her family to raise the issue with federal officials. John Knight, director of the L.G.B.T. Project of the American Civil Liberties Union of Illinois, which represented her, said concerns over the presence of transgender students in locker rooms "is a made-up issue."

"The kids who are most vulnerable are the transgender students," he said. "If a boy who's transgender is comfortable to be in a boys' restroom, he should be allowed to be there."

Catherine Lhamon, the Education Department's assistant secretary for civil rights, said it is possible to protect the rights of all students without forcing transgender students to use different facilities.

"The school's responsibility is to respect who that person is," Ms. Lhamon said. "And the school's responsibility is that they do not teach discrimination, but do teach civic engagement along with the three R's."

Transgender Students and 'Bathroom Laws' in South Dakota and Beyond

BY KATIE ROGERS | FEB. 25, 2016

THE SOUTH DAKOTA LEGISLATURE approved a bill this month that would require public school students to use bathrooms and other facilities that correspond to their biological sex, defined in the bill as "a person's chromosomes and anatomy as identified at birth."

Under the measure, schools would need to find other accommodations for transgender students, whose gender identity does not correspond with the biological sex they were born with. If the legislation is signed by Dennis Daugaard, the state's Republican governor, South Dakota will become the first state to enact such a law, and transgender students, their parents and their supporters criticize it as discriminatory.

On the other side of the debate, some schools say allowing transgender students to use the bathroom of their choice could violate the privacy of other students.

"I developed the bill because I don't want my four daughters to shower with people with male anatomy," Fred Deutsch, the Republican state representative behind the bill, told The Rapid City Journal.

ARE TRANSGENDER STUDENTS PROTECTED BY FEDERAL LAW?

Yes. In 2014, the Education Department's Office for Civil Rights issued guidance saying that transgender students are protected under Title IX, a federal law that prohibits sex-based discrimination in federally funded education programs. The guidance defines discrimination against transgender people as actions "based on gender identity or failure to conform to stereotypical notions of masculinity or femininity."

Still, schools have challenged the Education Department's mandate. In one notable example, a school district in Illinois was forced to find accommodations for a transgender student who wanted to use the girls' locker room, but only after the Education Department threatened to strip the district of its Title IX funding.

The district, Township High School District 211 in Palatine, Ill., maintained that its policy prohibiting the student from using the girls' locker room was not against the law, and said that the privacy concerns of 12,000 other students were also important.

HAVE OTHER PLACES TRIED TO ENACT 'BATHROOM LAWS'?

Yes. Debates over such measures have erupted in several states and cities, particularly in the past year. The local disputes highlighted a stark contrast with strides toward greater acceptance and exploration of gender identity in the mainstream, perhaps best illustrated by Caitlyn Jenner's coming out on the cover of Vanity Fair.

In some cases, the measures were anti-discrimination laws. For example, in Charlotte, N.C., on Monday, lawmakers passed a city ordinance that would allow transgender customers to use the bathroom of their choice, according to The Associated Press. Gov. Pat McCrory, a Republican, warned that the decision would create public safety issues.

Last year, voters in Houston repealed an ordinance banning discrimination based on several "protected characteristics," including gender identity. While sex and religion were among the other characteristics in the proposed ordinance, the vote against it seemed to focus on the prospect of transgender people in bathrooms corresponding with their gender identity, according to The Texas Tribune.

Other facilities, from the White House to the Utah Museum of Fine Arts in Salt Lake City, have created gender-neutral restrooms (and signage for them).

Schools in Illinois, California, Idaho, Maine, Nevada and Missouri have faced cases, and lawsuits, in which students felt discriminated against for not being able to use the bathrooms of their choosing. These disputes often stand in contrast with other moves that are seen as advancements, such as allowing transgender students to be called by their chosen name or participate in gendered sports.

Often, a transgender student and the student's supporters will call for the student to be able to use the bathroom of his or her choice. Parents sometimes respond by pulling their children out of school, as parents in Idaho did after a transgender girl was allowed to use the girls' bathroom. And sometimes, other students get involved: In Missouri, when a transgender girl fought to use the girls' locker room and bathroom last summer, her peers gathered outside the school to protest her.

In other cases, schools are adapting without attracting national attention: Miraloma Elementary School in San Francisco began making space for gender-neutral restrooms last year.

"We have students on the gender spectrum," the school said on its website. "Converting most of our bathrooms to gender neutral benefits all students of every grade level and creates a safe and supportive environment for all of our students."

HOW HAS THE TRANSGENDER COMMUNITY REACTED?

Supporters of the transgender community have protested the legislation in South Dakota on social media, mobilizing under the hashtags #HiFromSD and #HB1008 to share their thoughts.

Several famous supporters have also gotten involved. On Twitter, Ms. Jenner has shared an American Civil Liberties Union petition urging Mr. Daugaard to veto the bill. Laverne Cox, an actress and longtime advocate of transgender people, shared a photo on Instagram of Thomas Lewis, a transgender South Dakota student who said he often left school during his lunch break to use the bathroom at home.

"We should be creating safer, nurturing environments for our children, not more hostile ones," Ms. Cox said in her post.

IF SOUTH DAKOTA'S GOVERNOR SIGNS THE BILL, WILL LAWSUITS FOLLOW?

Most likely. The state law would conflict with federal rules already in place. Adam P. Romero, senior counsel and Arnold D. Kassoy scholar of law at the U.C.L.A. School of Law's Williams Institute, wrote in an email, "The South Dakota law, which looks to the student's sex assigned at birth and thus prohibits transgender students from using the restroom that corresponds to their gender identity, would clash with the Department of Education's interpretation of Title IX, and courts will be very likely required to resolve this conflict."

South Dakota Bill on Transgender Students' Bathroom Access Draws Ire

BY MITCH SMITH | FEB. 25, 2016

SIOUX FALLS, S.D. — For Thomas Lewis, a high school senior who plays trumpet in the marching band and works evenings at a grocery store, South Dakota's contentious debate over transgender rights is personal.

Mr. Lewis, 18, who came out as transgender last year, has been speaking out against a bill that would prohibit public school students from using a bathroom or locker room for a sex other than theirs at birth. If the bill is signed by Gov. Dennis Daugaard, a Republican, it will make South Dakota the first state to impose such a law.

Proponents of the legislation say it would help protect children and ensure everyone's privacy, but its passage has inserted South Dakota into the center of a national debate about transgender rights and access to restrooms and locker rooms.

It is among a number of bills addressing the rights of transgender people that are being pushed by conservative legislators in this state and others. Another South Dakota bill, which was shelved this week, would have required public agencies to accept only information on birth certificates, effectively preventing legal recognition of sex changes.

Mr. Lewis said the bathroom legislation, which was passed by the South Dakota Legislature last week, "creates more stigma," increases the risk of bullying and sends a message to transgender students: "You're so different, in a bad way, that you need your own bathroom, your own locker room, your own shower situation."

State Representative Fred Deutsch, the Republican who introduced the bill, said it was intended "to protect the innocence of children."

"How do we protect their minds and hearts and eyes while they're showering and changing?" said Mr. Deutsch, a former school board member from northeastern South Dakota.

In Houston, voters repealed an anti-discrimination ordinance last year that included transgender people after opponents seized on the message "No Men in Women's Bathrooms." In Missouri, high school students protested last year when a transgender girl requested to use the girls' locker room and restroom.

Individual school districts in places like California and Illinois have adopted rules barring transgender students from restrooms that correspond with their gender identity. Federal officials have intervened and threatened to cut off Title IX funds to districts that do not allow transgender students to use their preferred bathrooms and changing areas, though some conservatives have questioned the government's interpretation of that rule.

The South Dakota legislation would seem to put the state in conflict with the Obama administration's interpretation of the federal Title IX law, which prohibits discrimination on the basis of sex in any education program or activity that receives federal funds. Mr. Lewis said last week that he would probably continue to use the men's restroom at school even if Mr. Daugaard signed the bill. Even supporters of the legislation acknowledge that a school district will probably be sued if it becomes law.

"This bill would put schools in a very difficult situation, where they have to decide whether they want to comply with federal law or they're going to follow what their state is mandating," said Heather Smith, executive director of the American Civil Liberties Union of South Dakota, which opposes the bill.

Mr. Deutsch, the bill's sponsor, said he was unaware of major disputes over transgender bathroom access in his state and acknowledged that the bill was "entirely preventative." But he suggested that not enacting it could also lead to lawsuits, and that "in a small, rural state like this, there'd be an outrage from students" if a transgender youth were given full access to showering and changing facilities.

The bill has support from the Heritage Foundation, the Washington-based conservative research group, and the Roman Catholic bishops of South Dakota.

"The teaching of the Catholic Church is clear: One's gender, male or female, is determined by God and not a matter of personal choice," the bishops said in a statement last month. They added that the bill would respect "the innate dignity of all persons in our schools."

Mr. Deutsch said he felt "terrible that transgender children feel under siege," and noted that his bill would allow transgender students to request a separate accommodation if they did not want to use the bathroom corresponding with their sex at birth.

Mr. Lewis said the onus was on others to accept his identity as a man rather than on him to conform to their expectations, and noted that locked stall doors already ensured a layer of privacy. "Bathrooms don't need to change," he said. "People do."

In Watertown, high school students gathered more than 200 signatures for a petition saying the bathroom bill was discriminatory and should be voted down. And on the Rosebud Indian Reservation, where State Senator Troy Heinert once taught elementary school, Mr. Heinert said a transgender girl had attended classes years ago without any issue.

"Parents said, 'He dresses as a girl, he lives as a girl, he plays with girls,' " recalled Mr. Heinert, a Democrat who voted against the bill. "We made some accommodations at our school. Nobody cared. Everybody knew. We didn't make a mountain out of a molehill."

In neighboring Iowa, a bill that advanced recently would extend hate crime protections to transgender people. And in Minnesota, anti-discrimination protections were extended to transgender people more than 20 years ago.

South Dakota's bill has attracted the attention of transgender advocates nationally, some of whom have posted criticism of the bill and threats of a tourism boycott on social media with the hashtag "#HiFromSD," which was previously used to promote visiting the state.

Sarah Warbelow, legal director at the Human Rights Campaign, which promotes the rights of lesbian, gay, bisexual and transgender people, said bills like this were in part a backlash against victories for rights advocates on issues like same-sex marriage.

"For a very long time, many people accepted that they just had a right to discriminate against transgender people," Ms. Warbelow said. "This is a reaction to enforcement. It's also a reflection of better understanding that trans people exist."

Indeed, Mr. Daugaard, whose office said he had not decided whether to sign the bill, was quoted recently in the local news media as saying he was not aware of having met a transgender person. After reading that comment, Kendra Heathscott, a transgender woman from Sioux Falls, wrote in a letter to the state's largest newspaper, The Argus Leader, that she had known the governor as a child. Ms. Heathscott recalled Mr. Daugaard as a kind, accepting man and urged him to veto the bill.

Mr. Daugaard met with transgender rights advocates, including Mr. Lewis and Ms. Heathscott, on Tuesday. He told reporters on Thursday that he "saw things through their eyes" in that meeting, and that he was continuing to study the issue.

Mr. Lewis said that Mr. Daugaard had been "listening and asking us questions," though he said the governor had not indicated what he would do with the bill. It reached the governor's desk on Tuesday, a spokeswoman said, and he must act within five business days.

U.S. Directs Public Schools to Allow Transgender Access to Restrooms

BY JULIE HIRSCHFELD DAVIS AND MATT APUZZO | MAY 12, 2016

WASHINGTON — The Obama administration is planning to issue a sweeping directive telling every public school district in the country to allow transgender students to use the bathrooms that match their gender identity.

A letter to school districts will go out Friday, adding to a highly charged debate over transgender rights in the middle of the administration's legal fight with North Carolina over the issue. The declaration — signed by Justice and Education department officials — will describe what schools should do to ensure that none of their students are discriminated against.

It does not have the force of law, but it contains an implicit threat: Schools that do not abide by the Obama administration's interpretation of the law could face lawsuits or a loss of federal aid.

The move is certain to draw fresh criticism, particularly from Republicans, that the federal government is wading into local matters and imposing its own values on communities across the country that may not agree. It represents the latest example of the Obama administration using a combination of policies, lawsuits and public statements to change the civil rights landscape for gays, lesbians, bisexual and transgender people.

After supporting the rights of gay people to marry, allowing them to serve openly in the military and prohibiting federal contractors from discriminating against them, the administration is wading into the battle over bathrooms and siding with transgender people.

"No student should ever have to go through the experience of feeling unwelcome at school or on a college campus," John B. King Jr., the

ZACH GIBSON/THE NEW YORK TIMES

President Obama during a news conference at the White House last week.

secretary of the Department of Education, said in a statement. "We must ensure that our young people know that whoever they are or wherever they come from, they have the opportunity to get a great education in an environment free from discrimination, harassment and violence."

Courts have not settled the question of whether the nation's sex discrimination laws apply in matters of gender identity. But administration officials, emboldened by a federal appeals court ruling in Virginia last month, think they have the upper hand. This week, the Justice Department and North Carolina sued each other over a state law that restricts access to bathrooms, locker rooms and changing rooms. The letter to school districts had been in the works for months, Justice Department officials said.

"A school may not require transgender students to use facilities inconsistent with their gender identity or to use individual-user facilities when other students are not required to do so," according to the letter, a copy of which was provided to The New York Times.

A school's obligation under federal law "to ensure nondiscrimination on the basis of sex requires schools to provide transgender students equal access to educational programs and activities even in circumstances in which other students, parents, or community members raise objections or concerns," the letter states. "As is consistently recognized in civil rights cases, the desire to accommodate others' discomfort cannot justify a policy that singles out and disadvantages a particular class of students."

As soon as a child's parent or legal guardian asserts a gender identity for the student that "differs from previous representations or records," the letter says, the child is to be treated accordingly — without any requirement for a medical diagnosis or birth certificate to be produced. It says that schools may — but are not required to — provide other restroom and locker room options to students who seek "additional privacy" for whatever reason.

Attached to the letter, the Obama administration will include a 25-page document describing "emerging practices" that are in place in many schools around the country. Those included installing privacy curtains or allowing students to change in bathroom stalls.

In a blog post accompanying the letter, senior officials at the Justice and Education Departments said they issued it in response to a growing chorus of inquiries from educators, parents and students across the country, including from the National Association of Secondary School Principals, to clarify their obligations and "best practices" for the treatment of transgender students.

"Schools want to do right by all of their students and have looked to us to provide clarity on steps they can take to ensure that every student is comfortable at their school, is in an environment free of discrimination, and has an opportunity to thrive," wrote Catherine E. Lhamon, the assistant secretary of education for civil rights, and Vanita Gupta, the head of the Justice Department's Civil Rights Division.

Thomas Aberli, a high school principal in Louisville, Ky., said the new guidance would help administrators across the country who are trying to determine the best way to establish safe and inclusive schools. He said his school had little to work with when it drafted a policy that was put in place last year.

"What you don't do is go and tell a kid, 'You know, there is something so freakishly different about you that you make other people uncomfortable, so we're going to make you do something different'," said Mr. Aberli, who estimated that his school of 1,350 students had about six transgender children. "There's been no incident since its implementation. It's really just a nonissue in our school."

The White House has called North Carolina's law "meanspirited" and said this week that federal agencies were continuing a review of their policies on the treatment of transgender people while the administration waged its legal battle with the state.

President Obama condemned the law last month, saying it was partly the result of politics and "emotions" that people had on the issue.

"When it comes to respecting the equal rights of all people, regardless of sexual orientation, whether they're transgender or gay or lesbian, although I respect their different viewpoints, I think it's very important for us not to send signals that anybody is treated differently," Mr. Obama said at a news conference in London.

The struggle over the rights of transgender people has reverberated on the presidential campaign trail and become a defining issue in the final year of Mr. Obama's tenure, prompting boycotts of North Carolina by some celebrities and businesses that had planned to create jobs there. The fresh guidance to be issued Friday seemed certain to intensify that debate, and showed that Mr. Obama and his administration intend to press the issue of transgender rights aggressively as the legal challenge unfolds.

The Justice Department has for years made gay and transgender issues centerpieces of its civil rights agenda. Former Attorney General Eric H. Holder Jr. described that campaign as a continuation of the civil rights era that brought equal rights to African-Americans. And this week, Attorney General Loretta E. Lynch spoke passionately to transgender people as she cast the lawsuit against North Carolina in historic terms.

"We stand with you," she said. "And we will do everything we can to protect you going forward. Please know that history is on your side."

Some Republicans have defended North Carolina's law by arguing that it would be inappropriate to allow transgender women to use the same bathroom as young girls. Before ending his presidential bid last week, Senator Ted Cruz of Texas charged that Donald J. Trump, the presumptive Republican nominee, and Hillary Clinton, the likely Democratic nominee, "both agree that grown men should be allowed to use the little girls' restroom."

Transgender Directives for Schools Draw Reaction from Across the Country

BY CHRISTINE HAUSER | MAY 13, 2016

A TORRENT OF online reaction followed the release on Friday of federal guidance to public school districts in the United States that for the first time addresses how they should enforce the rights of transgender students.

The joint directive from the Department of Justice and the Department of Education says that schools must allow students to use bathrooms based on their gender identity and touches on issues including housing, locker rooms, pronouns and gender references on identity documents.

The measure, which is the Obama administration's latest to address the civil rights of gays, lesbians, bisexual and transgender people, has attracted both criticism and support, much of it reflecting bipartisan lines.

Representative Steve King, a Republican from Iowa, said the directive was "executive overreach." He told CSPAN: "And it's a topic we're likely to bring up in a future hearing before the task force that I chair."

In Texas, Lt. Gov. Dan Patrick told superintendents not to enact the directives: "We will not be blackmailed."

Rodney Cavness, a school superintendent in Port Neches, Tex., told 12 News: "He ain't my president and he can't tell me what to do. That letter is going straight to the paper shredder. I have five daughters myself and I have 2,500 girls in my protection. Their moms and dads expect me to protect them."

Nancy Pelosi, the Democratic leader, said on Twitter: "Thank you @USEDGov for standing up for transgender students by ensuring all students feel welcome and safe!"

Donald J. Trump, the presumptive Republican nominee, said on the "Today" show that he did not believe it was an issue for the federal government.

"Let the states decide. I think it's much better as a local issue. I don't think it's a federal issue where the federal government gets involved. And I see what's happening. It's become such a big situation. Everybody has to be protected and I feel strongly about that but you're talking about a tiny, tiny group of population."

Gov. Pat McCrory of North Carolina, who has sued the Justice Department in a dispute over public restroom access, said the executive branch "does not have the authority to be the final arbiter" on bathrooms, Colin Campbell, a reporter in North Carolina, wrote on Twitter quoting a copy of the governor's statement.

The key word "transgender" was trending on Twitter. It had been tweeted more than 44,000 times from early Friday morning until about noon, according to Dataminr data.

Mark Ruffalo, the Oscar winning actor, praised the move in a tweet, which read, "Bravo @POTUS! Obama administration to schools: Let transgender students go to the bathroom http://m.dailykos.com/stories/1526113"

The Transgender Law Center's executive director, Kris Hayashi, expressed gratitude: "Transgender students, like all students, just want to be able to go to school, be with their friends, and get an education without having to worry about being singled out and made to feel different."

Thousands of people wrote in response to the new directives in comments on The New York Times's Facebook page and on NYTimes.com.

"Regardless of the transgender issue, I have a problem with the President being able to authorize the 'loss of federal aid' to government bodies that behave contrary to his wishes," wrote Christian Miller of Saratoga, Calif.

"Thank you to the Obama administration for taking a stand against bigots and bullies. Children need support, love and understanding. For

Trans kids this is a vulnerable age. We don't need any more tragic deaths," wrote Michelle Franca on Facebook.

"It is not legal for the president to order there to be discrimination in public schools. If transgender people can choose their preferred bathroom regardless of their gender, then the same should apply to everyone who is not transgendered. Obama gets another one wrong," Chris Palsz wrote.

"I hope they sue the administration WHEN, not IF a case of sexual assault/voyeurism occurs. Children's rights and safety trump political correctness! The common sense thing to do is create another bathroom for whatever the heck a transwhatever identifies as, not let them go in the girls/boys bathrooms," Driena Sixto wrote.

Solace and Fury as Schools React to Transgender Policy

BY JACK HEALY AND RICHARD PÉREZ-PEÑA | MAY 13, 2016

DENVER — The Obama administration's directive Friday on the use of school bathrooms and locker rooms by transgender students intensified the latest fierce battle in the nation's culture wars, with conservatives calling it an illegal overreach that will put children in danger and advocates for transgender rights hailing it as a breakthrough for civil rights.

The policy drew a swift backlash from conservative politicians, groups and parents.

In Texas, Lt. Gov. Dan Patrick appealed to local school boards and superintendents not to abide by the directive, noting that there were just a few weeks left in the school year and time over the summer to fight the policy with legislation or legal action. "We will not be blackmailed," he said.

"I believe it is the biggest issue facing families and schools in America since prayer was taken out of public schools," Mr. Patrick, a Republican, said at a news conference. "Parents are not going to send their 14-year-old daughters into the shower or bathroom with 14-year-old boys. It's not going to happen."

With a jab at another job Mr. Patrick has held, Josh Earnest, the White House press secretary, said, "I think this does underscore the risk of electing a right-wing radio host to a statewide office."

Earlier in the day, the Justice and Education Departments sent a letter to school districts saying that students must be allowed to use the facilities that match the sex they identify as, even if that conflicts with their anatomical sex. For districts that refuse to comply, the directive carries the potential threat of legal action or the withholding of federal funds.

The administration had already taken that position in scattered cases around the country — from a school district in the Chicago suburb, to a district in rural Virginia to, most prominently, this week's lawsuit challenging a North Carolina state law — but Friday's directive was the most sweeping attempt yet to impose that view, turning it into a national issue.

A recent poll found that a majority of Americans opposed laws like North Carolina's that require transgender people to use facilities that match the sex listed on their birth certificates, though the survey did not specifically ask about schools and children. Republicans were evenly split, while Democrats and independents were strongly opposed to such requirements.

The events this week demonstrate how starkly views vary by region. The Massachusetts State Senate passed a bill that would allow transgender people to use the bathrooms conforming to their gender identities.

"The new guidance from the Obama administration on transgender youth in schools reaffirms a basic human right," said Chirlane McCray, the wife of Mayor Bill DeBlasio of New York City, which already has such a policy. "No child should face humiliation and embarrassment because of their gender identity, especially during such a private moment."

In Fort Worth, a deep divide became evident after the school district adopted a similar policy, prompting impassioned speeches and demonstrations from both sides at a school board meeting.

At the same time, eight states filed a brief siding with North Carolina in its legal fight with the administration. And in Fannin County, Ga., a sparsely populated area bordering North Carolina and Tennessee, hundreds of people marched to a school board meeting to insist that the district stick to traditional, anatomical standards in defining sex.

Steve Fallin, a pastor who participated in the march, spoke of a rising anger among many Christians who feel they are not being treated with respect, a fury that intensified Friday with news of the president's directive.

"What President Obama did with this letter, he just cranked up the heat on the pot just a few degrees too high," Mr. Fallin said. "I can tell you from what I saw last night, most of rural America, particularly the South, is right ready to just boil over."

Advocates on both sides said they suspect that most school districts did not have explicit policies defining gender. There are districts that allow transgender students to use the facilities that match their identities, and districts that prohibit it, but no definitive count of either group.

Jeremy Tedesco, senior counsel at the Alliance Defending Freedom, a conservative Christian legal group, argued that the administration was distorting a 1972 law requiring equal rights for women and girls in education, known as Title IX.

"The Obama administration has absolutely no legal authority to change what a statute means, and that's what they're doing," he said. "And they have complete and utter disregard for students' privacy and safety in these intimate settings."

Tim Moore, the Republican speaker of the North Carolina House, said, "We all have to wonder what other threats to common sense norms may come before the sun sets on the Obama administration."

Despite the federal directive and a civil rights complaint by the American Civil Liberties Union, the school district in Marion County, Fla., said it would not change its bathroom policy. "It's just an overreaching federal government that didn't follow the rules," said Nancy Stacy, a board member. "They're just bullying everybody."

But transgender people and groups that advocate for them praised the administration's action on Friday as a civil rights milestone.

Capri Culpepper, a transgender high school senior in Anderson, S.C., said the guidelines offered support to students like her, who can feel isolated and ostracized. She said school officials told her last year that she had to stop using the girl's restroom because it was making people uncomfortable, and allowed her to use a staff bathroom or one in the nurse's office.

"They were segregating me into this restroom that I didn't feel like I belonged in," she said.

Defenders of traditional gender norms say that changing them threatens the safety of women, allowing men claiming to be transgender women into women's bathrooms. Transgender advocates say that fear is misplaced, and the far greater danger is to transgender people.

"When you make a transgender student use a bathroom that is separate from all the other boys and girls you send a clear signal to the student body and to teachers that that student is so different that they can be treated worse," said Michael Silverman, executive director of the Transgender Legal Defense and Education Fund.

Jabari Lyles, president of a gay community center in Baltimore and the education manager for Baltimore's chapter of the Gay, Lesbian and Straight Education Network, applauded the directive, but said it would be an uphill battle to put in place.

"Hopefully, what this doesn't do is put transgender students more in danger because the law has taken a bold step on their side," he said.

Chad Griffin, president of the Human Rights Campaign, said, "This is a truly significant moment not only for transgender young people but for all young people, sending a message that every student deserves to be treated fairly and supported by their teachers and schools."

Transgender Bathroom Debate Turns Personal at a Vermont High School

BY ANEMONA HARTOCOLLIS | MAY 17, 2016

CHESTER, VT. — The way A.J. Jackson tells it, he kept his head ducked down and pretended to fiddle with his cellphone as he walked into the boys' bathroom and headed for a stall at Green Mountain Union High School here.

But the way some of his classmates see it, A.J. was still Autumn Jackson, a girl in boys' clothing, who had violated an intimate sanctum, while two boys were standing at a urinal, their private parts exposed.

"It's like me going into a girls' bathroom wearing a wig," Tanner Bischofberger, 15, a classmate of A.J. Jackson's, who was not one of those in the bathroom, said this week. "It's just weird."

A complaint about Mr. Jackson's using the boys' bathroom set off a protest by students advocating the right of their transgender classmate to use the bathroom of his choice. On Thursday, the schools superintendent announced a new practice at the high school allowing transgender students to use the sex-specific bathroom of their choice, rather than being encouraged to use a gender-neutral bathroom. The announcement came a day before the Obama administration's national directive was announced.

But this week, there was a counterprotest by students like Mr. Bischofberger wearing T-shirts showing the male and female figures commonly used to label bathrooms, over the words "Straight Pride."

Like much of the country, this rural school of 300 students in seventh through 12th grade, where everyone insists there were never any cliques, is divided over the bathroom issue, with the teenagers here carrying out a proxy culture war for their parents and the country. Still struggling to form opinions about what makes a civil society, they openly quote what they have heard their parents say about the merits or demerits of transgender bathrooms.

And the dispute has driven apart young people who grew up together and were once friends.

Some say the new rule opens the door to sexual predators disguised as someone they are not. Others say it just violates tradition. A society has rules for a reason, and this is one of those rules, that's just the way it is, they say.

But on a more basic level, students at Green Mountain are complaining that a small vocal minority of gay, lesbian and, as far as they know, one — or maybe two — transgender students among them are trampling on the rights of the majority to decide what the rules of conduct should be.

That idea of a minority's ruling unfairly is what motivated the father of one student to order the "Straight Pride" T-shirts online last week and send them to school with his daughter, who declined to be interviewed.

The T-shirt-wearing students say gay people are being celebrated at the expense of straight people.

"I just want to be clear: I accept everybody being proud," said Daniel Baldwin, a 17-year-old junior. Sitting at a table in the school hallway, a copy of "The Catcher in the Rye" open in front of him, he wore a "Straight Pride" shirt pulled over a shirt dedicated to Slayer, a thrash-metal band. "Everybody has the right to be who they are."

Mr. Baldwin said he thought people should use male or female bathrooms depending on what was written on their birth certificates. But he also said he would defend A.J. if someone tried to bully him for being transgender, or even for using the boys' bathroom. "I would step up for A.J.," he said. "We're Americans. We're supposed to be civil."

Listening to him, Mr. Jackson said he was dismayed by how they had been torn apart. "Oh, my God, we used to talk for hours about music," he said.

More broadly, the issue here has pitted resident against resident, often along social and economic lines. This is a place where big-city transplants wearing Birkenstocks and artsy jewelry mingle with working-class people in dirt-encrusted boots who know how to handle a shotgun and proudly inhabit the homes of their ancestors. Despite Vermont's image as a place of bucolic egalitarianism, home of the avowedly socialist candidate for president, tensions over privilege and tradition simmer just under the surface, and the bathroom wars have brought them to the fore.

"I go in and do my thing and leave, but I have a concern about child molesters and pedophiles," Joe Kopacz, 48, who runs a rock-crushing operation, said as he stopped into Lisai's Chester Market.

Society does not change on a dime, especially small-town society, said Deb Brown, a member of the Green Mountain Union High School board, speaking in MacLaomainn's, a pub and popular gathering spot that she owns with her husband. For people like her daughter, who was on girls' sports teams with A.J. when he was Autumn, this is intensely personal, not just philosophical.

"As we move forward as a community, there has to be compassion on both sides," Ms. Brown said. "He needs to understand that this has been 15 years that students have known him one way. It's obviously his choice, but maybe he should have respect for his classmates right now."

Mr. Jackson has gradually been making the transition from a vivacious girl with a big smile and long wavy locks to a husky boy with chopped hair dyed several shades of green, snakebite piercings in his lips and gauges embedded in his earlobes. His chest is visibly bound, and because he has not yet started taking male hormones — he plans to do that, and also to have "top surgery," he says — his face is smooth and still has feminine contours. He once thought he was lesbian, and is still attracted to girls.

His mother, Tracy, a case manager for children with developmental disabilities, and his father, Scott, a mechanical engineer, came to Vermont from Connecticut to try it out 20 years ago and stayed. They brought up A.J. and his older brother in a log cabin in the woods, where they raise chickens and ducks, including a duck named Bernie, for you know who.

"A typical American family," his mother said, smiling.

He was in sixth grade when he realized he was meant to be a boy, he said, and came out to the school last year in ninth grade, sending emails to teachers. When he entered Green Mountain in seventh grade, "I was using the female bathroom because, I really don't know, I was still kind of back and forth about my identity," Mr. Jackson said. "This year is the year I started using the men's bathroom, because I already felt like way more comfortable in who I was."

There were practical issues. When he had his period, he wondered if he should revert to the girls' bathroom, because there was no place to throw away his used tampons. But he had started feeling like an intruder in the girls' bathroom, and the single bathrooms were so far out of the way it was hard to get to class on time.

So he stuck with the boys' bathroom.

"I use a stall, and I wait till everybody's gone to get up and leave," Mr. Jackson said. "The guys, they look at me like I'm some kind of freak, or they're concerned or scared."

The only classmate who talks to him when he sees him in the bathroom is his childhood friend Connor Rose, a leader of the school's gay-straight alliance.

Mr. Jackson feels safe in the boys' bathroom at school, he said, whereas in public places, like Dunkin' Donuts, he is afraid to go to the men's restroom for fear of being attacked by straight men.

He said he understood the concerns of some of his classmates.

"There probably are some transgender people that are bad people, just like there are probably a whole bunch of gay people or straight people that are bad," he said.

He had been using the boys' bathrooms for less than a month — trying to go in during lunch or recess when he would not be noticed — when someone complained. No one knows for sure who complained, but a widespread rumor holds that it was a middle schooler.

Hank Mauti, a school board member and retired sawmill worker from Andover, said he wondered why Mr. Jackson would feel compelled to use a boys' bathroom when there were six single-use gender-neutral bathrooms in the school.

"What about the little boy that reported it?" asked Mr. Mauti's wife, Wanda, repeating the rumor, in an interview in their home, under a trophy of a moose that Mr. Mauti shot. "As far as I can tell, his discomfort hasn't been addressed."

Tom Ferenc, the principal, called Mr. Jackson's mother the night of the complaint and told her that he was going to ask A.J. to use the gender-neutral bathroom, she recalled. The next Monday, A.J. and about 30 supporters walked out of the school in protest. Three days later, the district announced the new policy.

Mr. Ferenc was happy to get some "clarity" about the proper policy, as he put it, and proud of his school. "It reminded me of Rosa Parks, honestly," he said.

Besides the "Straight Pride" T-shirt counterprotest, the decision has set off a storm of discussion, sometimes nasty on both sides, on Facebook. Also, someone taped a sign to a trash can this week that said, "Reserved for Mariah and Tanner," referring to Mariah Lique and Mr. Bischofberger, two student leaders of the counterprotest, who are dating.

Ms. Lique said that she and Mr. Bischofberger were just saying what a lot of other students think but are afraid to say because if they did, "you'd get hated."

"We're considered more conservative," she said. "Because we're outspoken," Mr. Bischofberger interjected, finishing her sentence.

Two of their favorite teachers are openly gay, they said, and the students misunderstand where they are coming from. "They see us as …" Mr. Bischofberger began, "hating their sexuality," Ms. Lique finished.

But that is not true, they said. Part of what troubles them is that Mr. Jackson is still anatomically female. "Autumn, A.J., whatever you call them, hasn't had any hormone or sex change yet," Mr. Bischofberger said. "This opens up opportunities for other kids to do stuff they're not supposed to."

While everyone seems to sympathize with the gay students, they seem to have a license to make him feel ostracized and attacked, and it hurts, Mr. Bischofberger said: "They're calling me a cisgendered, hypocritical homophobe."

JACK BEGG CONTRIBUTED RESEARCH.

How the Push to Advance Bathroom Rights for Transgender Americans Reached the White House

BY SHERYL GAY STOLBERG, JULIE BOSMAN, MANNY FERNANDEZ AND JULIE HIRSCHFELD DAVIS | MAY 21, 2016

THE PEOPLE OF Palatine, Ill., a middle-class suburb of Chicago marked by generic strip malls and tidy cul-de-sacs, had not spent much time debating the thorny questions of transgender rights. But in late 2013, a transgender high school athlete, so intent on defending her privacy that she is known only as Student A, took on her school district so she could use the girls' locker room.

After the federal Department of Education's Office for Civil Rights ruled in her favor last fall, the two sides cut a deal: Student A could use the locker room and the school would install private changing areas. Some in the community denounced the arrangement; others joined the American Civil Liberties Union of Illinois, which represented the girl, in declaring a victory for civil rights.

Now the whole nation is in a pitched battle over bathroom access, with the Obama administration ordering all public schools to allow transgender students to use the bathrooms of their choice. Across the country, religious conservatives are rebelling. On Friday, lawmakers in Oklahoma became the latest group to protest, proposing one measure to effectively overturn the order, and another calling for President Obama to be impeached over it.

How a clash over bathrooms, an issue that appeared atop no national polls, became the next frontier in America's fast-moving culture wars — and ultimately landed on the desk of the president — involves an array of players, some with law degrees, others still in high school.

The sweeping directive to public schools seemed to come out of nowhere. In fact, it was the product of years of study inside the government and a highly orchestrated campaign by advocates for gay and transgender people. Mindful of the role "Whites Only" bathrooms played in the civil rights battles of more than half a century ago, they have been maneuvering behind the scenes to press federal agencies, and ultimately Mr. Obama, to address a question that has roiled many school districts: Should those with differing anatomies share the same bathrooms?

The lobbying came to a head, according to people who were involved, in a hastily called April 1 meeting between top White House officials — led by Valerie Jarrett, Mr. Obama's senior adviser and one of his closest confidantes — and national leaders of the gay and transgender rights movement. North Carolina had just become the first state to explicitly bar transgender people from using the bathrooms of their choice.

"Transgender students are under attack in this country," said Chad Griffin, the president of the Human Rights Campaign, a Washington-based advocacy group that is active on the issue, summing up the message he sought to convey to Ms. Jarrett that day. "They need their federal government to stand up for them."

Ms. Jarrett and her team, he said, listened politely, but "did not reveal much," including the fact that a legal directive on transgender rights that had been in the works for months was about to be released.

When — or precisely how — Mr. Obama personally weighed in is not clear; the White House would not provide specifics. But two days before that meeting, scores of advocacy groups sent Mr. Obama a private letter, appealing to his sense of history as he nears the end of his presidency, in which he has already advanced gay and transgender rights on multiple fronts.

"Too many students — including every single transgender, intersex, and gender-nonconforming student in North Carolina — will go to sleep tonight dreading the next school day," the groups wrote, telling him that "your legacy will be defined by the tone you have set and the personal leadership you have shown on these issues."

The dispute in Palatine came amid increasing confusion for school districts over how to handle questions about bathroom access for transgender students. Officials at the Department of Education said it had received hundreds of requests for guidance — so many that advocates for gay and transgender rights, frustrated by the Obama administration's failure to issue specific policy guidelines, decided to act on their own.

In August, several groups seeking protection for transgender people — including the Human Rights Campaign, the National Education Association and the National Center for Lesbian Rights — issued a 68-page guide for schools, hoping to provide a blueprint for the White House.

At the Department of Education, Catherine E. Lhamon, 44, a former civil rights litigator who runs the agency's Office of Civil Rights — and has made aggressive use of a federal nondiscrimination law known as Title IX — was taking the lead. The department's ruling in favor of Student A in November was the first time it had found any school district in violation of civil rights over transgender issues.

For Student A, the federal intervention has been life changing. Her mother, who requested anonymity to protect the privacy of her daughter, said she was close to finishing her junior year and had just gone to the prom with a group of friends. (She wore a "nice, expensive dress" with a lot of sparkles, her mother said.) Student A is starting to think about which college she might attend.

"She's in her own teenaged world right now," her mother said.

The ruling in Palatine reverberated across the Midwest. In the South Dakota Legislature, Republicans were so alarmed by the situation in Palatine that, in February, they passed a measure restricting bathroom access for transgender students — similar to the one that later became law in North Carolina. Opponents sent transgender South Dakotans to meet with Gov. Dennis Daugaard, a Republican, and they believe that influenced his veto of the bill.

Among the visitors was Kendra Heathscott, who was 10 when she first met Mr. Daugaard, then the executive director of a social services organization that treats children with behavioral problems. In his office to lobby against the bathroom measure, she reintroduced herself. "He remembered me as a little boy," she said.

In Wisconsin last year, another Republican-sponsored bathroom bill began to work its way through the Legislature, but was beaten back by transgender rights activists, many of them teenagers.

In rural north-central Florida, a retired veterinarian and cattle rancher named Harrell Phillips was alarmed one evening in March, when his 17-year-old son reported over dinner that he had encountered a transgender boy in the high school bathroom.

"I marched myself down to the principal," said Dr. Phillips, who believes that "you are born into a sex that God chose you to be."

The principal, and later the school superintendent, citing advice from lawyers, said there was nothing they could do. So Dr. Phillips turned to his best friend, a lawyer in Jacksonville, who introduced him to Roger Gannam of Liberty Counsel, an Orlando-based Christian organization. Mr. Gannam represented Kim Davis, the Kentucky clerk jailed for refusing to issue same-sex marriage licenses last year.

Mr. Gannam had just helped block a proposed anti-discrimination ordinance in Jacksonville, with an argument religious conservatives have been lately using to powerful effect: It would endanger women and young girls by allowing men — and even sexual predators — to pose as transgender and enter women's bathrooms.

Ocala, where Dr. Phillips's son attends school, is now embroiled in a fight much like the one that engulfed Palatine. The school board, at Mr. Gannam's prodding, voted in April to require transgender students to use bathrooms that correspond with their biological sex.

One transgender young man there has been suspended for using the boys' bathroom. The A.C.L.U. of Florida sued the day before the White House issued its directive, and last Sunday night, transgender activists and their allies held a strategy session in a church — with a sheriff's deputy standing guard outside because attendees feared for their safety.

"It's separate but equal, so they might as well put black and white up on the bathrooms, too," said Beth Miller, the mother of 17-year-old Mathew Myers, formerly Madison, an R.O.T.C. student in Ocala who came out as transgender this fall by asking his sergeant to permit him to switch from a women's uniform to one for men. The sergeant accommodated Mathew on the uniform, but the school required him to use the gender-neutral bathroom in the nurse's office.

"I go to the guy's bathroom all the time out in public, and no one cares," Mathew said.

Dr. Phillips, who like many Americans was not focused on the issue until recently, vows to take his fight to the Supreme Court. He believes that Mr. Obama "should be impeached" and is furious at "the liberal left trying to push this down our throats."

Though North Carolina was the first state to adopt a law explicitly barring all transgender people from using public facilities of their choice, many say the current debate has its roots in Houston. In November 2015, voters there repealed the city's anti-discrimination measure, after a campaign in which the law's opponents boiled their message down to a five-word slogan. It appeared on yard signs, T-shirts, banners, and ominous ads on TV, radio and the Internet: "No Men in Women's Bathrooms."

More than 200 cities across the United States had adopted similar anti-discrimination laws by the time Houston went to the polls; Minneapolis expanded civil rights protections to transgender people back in 1975. But in Houston, the vote took place less than five months after the Supreme Court victory for same-sex marriage. Social conservatives were energized.

Religious conservatives say that broad civil rights protections for transgender people are unnecessary — a solution to a problem that, they argue, does not exist. Jeremy Tedesco, the lead counsel for Alliance Defending Freedom, an Arizona-based conservative advocacy group, argues that "when it comes to locker rooms and restrooms, separating the sexes is a matter of common decency."

The repeal of the Houston ordinance rattled national gay rights leaders.

"I think they have now created a campaign in a box that we are going to see shipped from city to city and state to state," Mr. Griffin, of the Human Rights Campaign, said in an interview at the time.

Mr. Griffin was correct; Alliance Defending Freedom has a website, www.safebathrooms.org, that went live two weeks ago, and its video has been viewed more than 300,000 times.

But the Human Rights Campaign and its allies have a playbook of their own, one patterned after their strategy for marriage equality, in which they fought the battle for acceptance state by state. After the defeat in Houston, their next targets were Jacksonville, Fla., and Charlotte, N.C. — Southern cities where the advocates worked aggressively to elect politicians who would push the cause of gay and transgender rights.

In Charlotte, an anti-discrimination ordinance failed in February 2015; after that, the Human Rights Campaign and other gay rights leaders poured money into a new organization — Turnout Charlotte. The goal was "to identify and support and ask candidates, 'Where are you on this issue?' " said LaWana Mayfield, an openly gay City Council member.

With heavy backing from the activists, three new council members were elected last fall, tilting the balance on the council, which passed the anti-discrimination ordinance in February. Religious conservatives, who had adopted the "No Men in Women's Bathrooms" message from Houston, were taken aback.

"It's outrageous to have a big Washington, D.C.-based organization come into the state to influence the public policy of a major city," said Tami Fitzgerald, the executive director of the North Carolina Values Coalition, an advocacy group.

Republicans in the legislature responded with the so-called bathroom bill, which Gov. Pat McCrory signed into law on March 23. Nine days later, the advocates had their audience with Ms. Jarrett. The

North Carolina law, they argued behind closed doors, had created an untenable conflict.

"The schools were put in this weird situation by Governor McCrory," said Mara Keisling, the executive director of the National Center for Transgender Equality, who was at the meeting. "And it just sped this whole thing up."

MATT APUZZO CONTRIBUTED REPORTING.

How High School Students See the Transgender Bathroom Issue

BY THE NEW YORK TIMES | MAY 18, 2016

WHEN THE OBAMA administration directed public schools on Friday to accommodate transgender students by ensuring that they may use school bathrooms and locker rooms of their choice, the latest battle in the nation's culture wars became even more contentious. Conservatives called the action an illegal overreach that will put children in danger. Advocates for transgender rights hailed it as a breakthrough for civil rights.

High school students from around the country shared their thoughts with The New York Times on Facebook. Their opinions ranged from anger to joy, and they offered a glimpse into how students are experiencing the issue in their schools and neighborhoods.

THE RIGHT DIRECTION

The Obama administration has taken significant steps in the right direction in social reform throughout its almost eight-year tenure, and this is just adding to its legacy. The United States was built on "freedom and justice for all," and discriminatory laws against transgender students simply disregard not just the Constitution, but the well-being of U.S. citizens. We live in 2016, and acceptance of everyone of every creed, race, sexuality, gender and background is not only a reflection of the time that we live in, but a necessity in American society.

ZOE ALLEN, 16, DALLAS

IT SHOULD BE UP TO THE SCHOOLS

It's a decision that should be left for the school's administration and board to decide. Also, it shouldn't be a reason to pull out federal funding if schools choose not to follow this law.

It's also up to Congress to write the laws, not the executive department.

JOSH BOOHER, 18, COLUMBIA, PA.

GIRLS DESERVE PRIVACY

1) I don't think it is the federal government's job to dictate what each school district does with its students. That is extreme government overreach, and it sets a bad precedent for the future.

2) I think that it is endangering females by opening the doors for any man who wants to enter locker rooms and restrooms where females are. I am not saying that transgender people will be the ones committing crimes; however, these laws and orders will allow any guy who wants to to enter these previously all-female spaces without being restricted by law. If schools want to provide a gender neutral restroom or space where transgender people can go, that is one thing, but eliminating any place where girls can go and have privacy from men is a very bad policy.

GRACE DRIGGERS, 17, SOUTH CAROLINA

THIS IS TERRIBLE

It is first of all not the federal government's job to determine this for every school, and to be 100 percent honest, this makes me as a female very uncomfortable. This liberal push for equality in virtually EVERYTHING is beyond ridiculous. You are given a gender, and whether you agree with it or not, you go to the bathroom you are assigned — not the one you determine. Mr. Obama, this is terrible, and for everyone out there that says this is a step for a safer environment, you are very, very mistaken.

ABBEY MORGAN, PARRISH, ALA.

PESSIMISTIC ABOUT THE OUTCOME

While I agree with the Obama administration in general and am an advocate for transgender rights, I'm pessimistic about the outcome. Schools that oppose challenging the gender binary will continue to do so, as they probably already resent the fast pace of social change and left-leaning federal government. In fact, schools with conservative administrations may be even more anti-trans in defiance. More open-minded, progressive schools probably have listened to student input in allowing transgender students to use the appropriate bathrooms and don't need the federal government's advice. All in all, this decision seemed like it was made for show; however, I agree with it and its significance is in its empowerment of and official solidarity with transgender students. It gives them a voice.

JENNY XU, 16, NEW YORK

A DISTRACTION FROM 'REAL ISSUES'

As a high schooler, I honestly couldn't care less which bathroom somebody uses if they're using whichever one matches their gender identification. I believe that the whole freakout on this issue is a ploy to distract people from the real issues that face us, like childhood poverty, undue corporate influence in politics and income inequality.

ANDREW FIGUEIREDO, 18, WICHITA, KAN.

WE ARE THRILLED

I'm a high schooler and the co-president of the Gay Straight Alliance at my school. I 100 percent think that this is a step in the right direction. We have been fighting for this right at my school for years and are very pleased that it is being addressed federally. We are thrilled that this will make our school a safer and more comfortable place for students to learn (and relieve themselves) regardless of their gender identity.

ROBBIE GOLDBERG, 16, FRAMINGHAM, MASS.

THIS IS A NON-PROBLEM

This is long overdue and especially appropriate. Being friends with many trans people myself, I find it nonsensical that conservatives will make up any excuse to oppose these laws, because in reality, they do not understand trans people, they do not want to and, as the word conservative implies, they are afraid of any kind of social progress. It is so easy to forget that there was extreme backlash to desegregation as well as women attending class, but the right for transgender people to use whichever bathroom they associate their identity with does indeed align with civil rights and social progress. There will be clamor, but the noise will die down eventually as people will realize this is a non-problem.

CHRISTIAN MIXSON, 18, GULF SHORES, ALA.

A Transgender Student Won Her Battle. Now It's War.

BY ANEMONA HARTOCOLLIS | APRIL 2, 2017

PALATINE, ILL. — Tall and sylphlike, an athlete with delicate features and a blond topknot, she changes clothes behind a privacy curtain in the girls' locker room at her high school. But just being allowed to set foot in that locker room was a huge victory for the girl. She is transgender.

She graduates in May — but the war over how to accommodate transgender students is far from over in her Chicago suburb.

A new legal challenge is making its way through the courts. And a coalition of insurgent school board candidates, an evangelical church and conservative parents are looking to reshape district policy. The goal: preventing transgender girls and boys from sharing the bathrooms and locker rooms of their choice with other girls and boys, on the grounds that they are "the opposite biological sex." Their presence, the opponents argue, violates community standards of decency.

They cast the issue as one of basic modesty, but the transgender student says it goes far deeper than that.

"Really, nobody's getting naked," said the girl, who is identified as Student A in court papers and asked not to be named to protect her privacy. "This fear that trans people exist and should not have the right to exist. That's the driving force here."

The school board election is set for Tuesday, only days after lawmakers in North Carolina, mired in a battle of its own, repealed a state law restricting bathroom use in public buildings. In February, after a dispute among his own cabinet officials, President Trump reversed federal protections allowing transgender students to use the bathrooms of their choice, leaving those decisions to state and local authorities. That in turn prompted the Supreme Court not to take what advocates had hoped would be a defining transgender bathroom case.

SALLY RYAN FOR THE NEW YORK TIMES

After one transgender student's victory at a high school district near Chicago, more cases are in the wings, including that of a transgender girl, above, identified as N.S., who has filed a discrimination complaint with the state.

Student A has been a pioneer in Township High School District 211, which covers five schools in relatively affluent communities northwest of Chicago that have a patchwork of ad hoc policies for transgender students. She filed a complaint with the civil rights office of the federal Department of Education in 2013 that resulted in a 2015 settlement allowing her to use the girls' locker room at William Fremd High School, in Palatine (and at other schools during school activities). The school had already been quietly allowing her to use the girls' bathroom.

But that agreement, essentially a contract between the district and the federal government, applies only to one person: Student A. It will expire when she graduates, making the district's future policy unclear. Waiting in the wings: two transgender boys known as Student B, now in junior high, and Student C, a freshman at another high school, and a transgender girl identified as N.S. who has filed a state discrimination complaint.

The township district settlement was one of several federal agreements on transgender students' rights made under the Obama administration across the country in places like Summerville, S.C., and Broadalbin, N.Y.

The repercussions are still playing out here. There is a slate of three insurgent candidates who oppose the district's transgender practices, Ralph Bonatz, Katherine David and Jean Forrest, in the school board elections. The candidates call themselves Parents With Purpose, and if they win, they will probably tip the balance of the seven-member school board to their side.

In a campaign flier, the candidates said they would not allow restroom access "to students of the opposite biological sex." At a recent candidates' forum, Ms. David said that she would represent "our community's beliefs and values." Mr. Bonatz, describing himself as a "regular guy," said the district should not be "compromising the well-being and dignity of 99 percent of the students."

James Pittman Jr., pastor of New Hope Community Church, an evangelical congregation of about 50 active members in Palatine, has become a regular, along with members of his church, at school board meetings and candidates' forums where transgender policy is discussed.

Pastor Pittman has become a particularly effective foil against the argument often made that the transgender rights movement is heir to the civil rights movement. "I am black; my family members are black," he said in an interview in his church. "None of my family members nor friends would equate this movement to the civil rights movement. Matter of fact, that's an insult."

"We didn't choose to be black," he said, "and no matter what choice we make in the future, guess what? We're still going to be black."

A letter from the church says: "God created two distinct and complementary sexes in the very biology of the human race. A biological male is never female or vice versa."

Many of the community members who oppose the school district's transgender practices make a point of referring to transgender students by their birth sex, not by the sex that they identify with or that, in some instances, is written on their official documents. To them, Student A is a "he," not a "she."

The battle is also taking place in the courtroom. More than 50 families have signed on to a lawsuit filed in Federal District Court by the Alliance Defending Freedom, a conservative Christian advocacy group based in Arizona, arguing that district policy toward Student A violates students' right to privacy. They say that girls in the locker room are in a constant state of anxiety over the possibility that they will see Student A undressed, or that she will see them.

The American Civil Liberties Union has taken up the other side.

Dan Harrington, one of the plaintiffs, put his daughter, Sarah, in a Christian school in the fall rather than send her to a District 211 high school. "Regardless of what he thinks he is, he's still a male," Mr. Harrington said of Student A.

Like many of the opponents, Mr. Harrington and his daughter have not met the transgender students they are talking about. Sarah suspects, but is not sure, that one of the younger transgender boys was in her Girl Scout troop.

They say they are sympathetic to the students, whom the plaintiffs' lawyer, Gary McCaleb, describes as "sincerely confused." But, Mr. Harrington said, "we have a lifestyle that we want to live, a modest lifestyle, a wholesome lifestyle."

Referring to Student A, Sarah said, "He can do whatever he wants to do; it's his life." But her father said that people "do not want to pay taxes for this particular violation of people's rights."

Another plaintiff, Vicki Wilson, said she was acting purely on principle, not out of any personal hostility. "I have a daughter who — can't get her into a dress for the life of me," she said.

Girls who complained, she said, were "belittled and bullied." And she said she worried that some girls who had been sexually abused would have their trauma rekindled by transgender students in the locker room.

Student A said the fuss had been magnified by parents. Her classmates, she said, have long perceived her as feminine. She always liked jewelry and began wearing girls' jeans in sixth grade.

"They almost create this fictitious being," she said. "When you humanize the issue, it becomes a nonissue." Most people, she said, "forget I'm even trans."

At her school, her identity is an open secret. At the candidates' forum, Bradley Posdal, 19, a college freshman, sat in a row near the front. He graduated from Fremd last year and attended the forum because he wanted to be an "informed voter," he said.

But it was often hard for him to tell which candidate stood where on the transgender issue because both sides seemed to be speaking in code. "They repeated the word 'privacy' a lot — and 'dignity,'" Mr. Posdal said.

Yes, he said, he knows Student A. He has since middle school, where she was bullied. And, he said with a smile, they attend the same church. "At least among my friend group," he said, "it's pretty well accepted that nobody really cares."

CHAPTER 3

Gavin Grimm

In the debate over bathroom access in schools, one student's story came to represent the heart of the issue. This was the case of Gavin Grimm, a 17-year-old transgender student from Virginia. After Grimm came out while a high school sophomore, the school board issued a ruling preventing Grimm from using the boy's bathroom. With the help of the American Civil Liberties Union, Grimm sued his school, and a several-year-long court battle began that reached its resolution in the Supreme Court during the early months of the Trump administration.

For Transgender Americans, Legal Battles Over Restrooms

BY THE NEW YORK TIMES | JULY 27, 2015

GAVIN GRIMM sat quietly in the audience last November as dozens of parents at a school board meeting in Gloucester County, Va., demanded that he be barred from using the boys' restrooms at school. They discussed the transgender boy's genitals, expressed concern that he might expose himself and cautioned that being in a men's room would make the teenager vulnerable to rape. One person called him a "freak."

When Gavin, 16, got his turn at the podium, he was remarkably composed. "I didn't ask to be this way," Gavin said. "All I want to do is be a normal child and use the restroom in peace."

On Monday, Judge Robert Doumar of Federal District Court in Virginia is scheduled to consider whether the school board's decision to

DAMON WINTER/THE NEW YORK TIMES

Gavin Grimm

prohibit Gavin from using the male restroom is unlawful discrimination. The case addresses one of the main unresolved battles in the fight for transgender equality.

A favorable decision for the student would be the first time a federal court has ruled that refusing transgender students access to proper restrooms is discriminatory. Any other outcome would reinforce cruel policies that deny dignity to some of the most vulnerable students and subject them to more bullying and stigmatization.

Access to public restrooms has been a divisive issue in past civil rights struggles. During the 1950s, African-Americans challenged Jim Crow laws that barred them from so-called white restrooms.

In the following decade, as more women joined the labor force, they had to fight to get employers to provide restrooms in workplaces that had historically been dominated by men. In the 1980s, when advocates for Americans with disabilities began getting traction in their quest for equal access to public accommodations, many questioned the cost and burden of building special restroom facilities.

It may seem inconceivable today that people on the forefront of those struggles were dismissed, mocked and shunned for years. Yet each was a hard-fought victory.

The debate over which public restrooms transgender people and those who are gender-nonconforming should be allowed to use has been brewing for years. Federal agencies have issued sensible guidelines in recent years for government workers and private employers. Last month, for instance, the Occupational Safety and Health Administration urged employers to allow workers to use restrooms that "correspond with their gender identity."

Some states and jurisdictions, including New York State, have adopted good guidelines for schools, while others have vague rules or none at all. The issue has generated heated debate in many communities across the country. In the absence of clear guidelines, many educators, parents and school board members have taken alarmist positions, suggesting that allowing transgender students to use the restroom of their choice would enable predators or make them easy prey for sexual assault.

"I have seen absolutely no empirical evidence, anything that comes close to any factual basis for either of those concerns," said Carlos Ball, a law professor at Rutgers University who has studied the history of policies regarding access to public restrooms. "On the other hand, there is a plethora of reports of transgender people being physically assaulted, verbally abused and harassed for being quote-unquote in the wrong bathroom."

Federal civil rights officials first addressed the issue in 2013, when they sided with a male transgender student in California who had been forced to change in an isolated facility for gym class and use a restroom that was far from his classrooms. Those rules were repealed in a settlement between the school district and the government.

Only a handful of cases have been brought in federal courts. In March, a District Court judge in Pennsylvania ruled against a student who was expelled from the University of Pittsburgh for using the men's room, preposterously concluding that the student had no right to do so because he was admitted as a female.

Some state legislators have eagerly entered the debate. A controversy at a Kentucky high school, which allowed a transgender girl to use the girls' restroom, prompted a Republican lawmaker to introduce a bill earlier this year that would have forced people in the state to use public restrooms according with the gender on their birth certificates.

Lawmakers in Florida, Minnesota and Texas have introduced similar "bathroom bills," which transgender activists have fought with a smart social media campaign — #WeJustNeedToPee. They showed how incongruous transgender men and women looked, standing next to non-transgender people in the restrooms lawmakers were insisting they use. None of those bills passed.

Gavin's lawsuit, which was filed by the American Civil Liberties Union, is one of two cases with similar facts currently before federal judges. The other was filed by a high school student in Michigan who was ostracized and barred from using the proper restroom.

The Department of Justice has submitted filings supporting both plaintiffs. The plaintiffs and federal officials argue that preventing transgender students from using restrooms that match their gender identity is a violation of Title IX, a federal law that bars discrimination based on gender in schools that receive federal funding. The Justice Department's statement of interest in Gavin's case notes that singling out transgender students makes it more likely that they will be bullied and harassed.

Before coming out as transgender in April 2014, Gavin wrestled with depression and anxiety. After he confided in his mother, who was supportive, he sought medical treatment for gender dysphoria and legally changed his name. He began the last school year as Gavin, with little notice at first. Initially, in consultation with his principal and teachers, he decided to use the nurse's restroom in school, rather than a gender-specific one, because he wanted to see how classmates would react to his transition.

Soon, though, feeling that most students were supportive or unfazed, he received permission to use the boys' room, and did so for seven weeks last fall without any problem. But when word of this reached parents in the community, many were incensed. In response, a Gloucester County school board member, Carla Hook, introduced a resolution in November stipulating that access to locker rooms and restrooms "shall be limited to the corresponding biological genders, and students with gender identity issues shall be provided an alternative appropriate private facility."

Her motion passed by a 6-to-1 vote after several parents threatened to vote school board members out of office if they sided with Gavin. That decision was met with resounding applause. "To hear a lot of people clapping and cheering for my failure was very upsetting," said Gavin, who aspires to go to college far from his community and become a neuroscientist. "I was in a room full of adults, and it felt vicious."

Since then, Gavin has tried to use the nurse's restroom at school as infrequently as possible, which has caused urinary tract infections. The ordeal has made him a pariah to many in his community. Judge Doumar has an opportunity to end blatant discrimination by ruling against the school board. Gavin's lawyers are seeking an injunction that would restore his right to use the proper restroom before school starts in September. A final ruling in the case may take several months.

In the meantime, the Department of Education, which has supported transgender students in individual lawsuits, should issue detailed across-the-board guidelines to all schools and universities. By doing so, it would help students in hostile communities who are having to wage humiliating fights for a basic right.

Supreme Court to Rule in Transgender Access Case

BY ADAM LIPTAK | OCT. 28, 2016

WASHINGTON — The Supreme Court on Friday entered the national debate over transgender rights, announcing that it would decide whether a transgender boy may use the boys' bathroom in a Virginia high school.

The court is acting just a year after it established a constitutional right to same-sex marriage, as state laws and federal actions on transgender rights have prompted a welter of lawsuits. In taking the case, the court signaled that it may move more quickly in the area of transgender rights than it has in expanding gay rights.

The public debate has been ignited, in part, by a North Carolina law that requires transgender people to use bathrooms in government buildings that correspond with the gender listed on their birth certificates, a statute that has drawn protests, boycotts and lawsuits.

The case revolves around how the Obama administration is entitled to interpret a federal regulation under a 1972 law that bans discrimination "on the basis of sex" in schools that receive federal money. The legal question is whether it can also ban discrimination based on gender identity.

The Department of Education said last year that schools "generally must treat transgender students consistent with their gender identity." In May, the department went further, saying that schools could lose federal money if they discriminate against transgender students.

That left school districts grappling with how to treat transgender students. In August, a federal judge in Texas blocked Obama administration guidelines on restroom access for such students.

The case the Supreme Court agreed to hear concerns Gavin Grimm, who was designated female at birth but identifies as male. He attends Gloucester High School in southeastern Virginia.

DAMON WINTER/THE NEW YORK TIMES

Gavin Grimm is suing his Virginia school district to use the boys' bathroom, which corresponds with his gender identity.

For a time, school administrators allowed Mr. Grimm, 17, to use the boys' bathroom, but the local school board later adopted a policy that required students to use the bathrooms and locker rooms for their "corresponding biological genders." The board added that "students with gender identity issues" would be allowed to use private bathrooms.

The American Civil Liberties Union, which represents Mr. Grimm, told the justices that "girls objected to his presence in the girls' restrooms because they perceived him to be male." The group's brief said requiring Mr. Grimm to use a private bathroom had been humiliating and had, quoting him, "turned him into 'a public spectacle' before the entire community, 'like a walking freak show.'"

Mr. Grimm, the brief said, "avoids drinking liquids and tries not to urinate during the school day" and has, as a consequence, "developed painful urinary tract infections and felt distracted and uncomfortable in class."

In a statement issued on Friday, Mr. Grimm said: "I never thought that my restroom use would ever turn into any kind of national debate. The only thing I ever asked for was the right to be treated like everyone else."

He continued: "While I'm disappointed that I will have to spend my final school year being singled out and treated differently from every other guy, I will do everything I can to make sure that other transgender students don't have to go through the same experience."

Speaking of the Supreme Court's decision, Shannon Minter, the legal director of the National Center for Lesbian Rights, said: "This is one of the most important days in the history of the transgender movement. The outcome of this case is likely to shape the future of that movement in ways that will resonate for a very long time."

Gary McCaleb, a lawyer with Alliance Defending Freedom, which filed a brief supporting the school board in Virginia, said, "Schools have a duty to protect the privacy and safety of all students."

"In light of the right to bodily privacy, federal law should not be twisted to require that a male be given access to the girls' facilities, or a female to the boys' facilities," he said.

After Mr. Grimm challenged the school board's bathroom policy in court last year, a divided panel of the United States Court of Appeals for the Fourth Circuit, in Richmond, Va., ruled the policy unlawful. A trial judge then ordered school officials to let Mr. Grimm use the boys' bathroom.

A 1975 regulation adopted under the 1972 law, Title IX, allowed schools to provide "separate toilet, locker rooms and shower facilities on the basis of sex." The Fourth Circuit said that it was ambiguous and that the Education Department's interpretation of it was entitled to "controlling weight."

A 4-to-4 tie in the Virginia case — Gloucester County School Board v. G.G., No. 16-273 — would leave that decision in place but set no national precedent. In agreeing to hear the case, the justices set aside their recent caution in adding cases to their docket while the court is reduced to eight members.

The justices may be hoping they will have a new member to replace Antonin Scalia, who died in February, in time for the argument in the case early next year.

The court also agreed to decide whether states may bar registered sex offenders from using Facebook and other social media.

That case, Packingham v. North Carolina, No. 15-1194, concerns a North Carolina law that makes it a crime for registered sex offenders to use Facebook, Twitter and many other sites that allow the exchange of information and do not limit their membership to adults.

The law was challenged by Lester Packingham, a registered sex offender who was convicted of violating it after posting an account of having a traffic ticket dismissed. “God is good,” he wrote on Facebook.

Mr. Packingham, who had pleaded guilty in 2002 to taking indecent liberties with a minor when he was a 21-year-old student, said the law violated the First Amendment.

A North Carolina appeals court agreed, saying the law “arbitrarily burdens all registered sex offenders by preventing a wide range of communication and expressive activity unrelated to achieving its purported goal” of protecting minors.

In a 4-to-2 ruling, the North Carolina Supreme Court reversed the decision, saying that Mr. Packingham’s Facebook post was not entitled to heightened First Amendment protection because it was conduct rather than speech.

In urging the United States Supreme Court to review his case, Mr. Packingham argued that the “startling assertion” that his post amounted to conduct and not speech was at odds with “precedent and common sense.”

Trump Will Lose the Fight Over Bathrooms for Transgender Students

OPINION | BY RIA TABACCO MAR | FEB. 23, 2017

ON WEDNESDAY EVENING, the Departments of Education and Justice, at the direction of President Trump, withdrew important guidance that required schools to treat transgender boys and girls like other boys and girls under Title IX, the 1972 federal law that prohibits sex discrimination in education.

In a one-and-a-half-page letter, the government unceremoniously retreated from a position — that transgender students may not be excluded from restrooms and locker rooms that match their gender identity — that the Department of Education had held for at least four years. Despite those years of experience, the government claims that it needs to "further and more completely consider the legal issues involved."

But there is nothing new about the idea that sex discrimination includes discrimination against transgender people. To the contrary, courts have repeatedly reached that conclusion over the past 15 years in decisions that involve prisons, banks, the workplace and, yes, schools. That's because it's impossible to take into account someone's transgender status or gender identity — their internal sense of being male, female or something else — without taking into account their sex. Indeed, transgender people are defined by the fact that their gender identity does not match the sex given to them at birth.

By insisting that more study is warranted to decide whether transgender students should be treated fairly, the government has sent a deeply disturbing message to transgender students that they are less than other students and unworthy of protection.

That would be a damaging thing for the Department of Education to do to anyone. But it is especially troubling here, given that transgender students already are subject to more violence and harassment — both by other children and by adults — than their peers. These obstacles help explain why many transgender students drop out of school, why nearly half of transgender children have considered suicide and why at least a quarter of them have attempted it. What's more, discrimination in schools has far-reaching and lifelong consequences for transgender people — psychologically and financially.

Although the letter notes that the law protects transgender students, like all students, from discrimination, bullying and harassment, requiring transgender students to use separate facilities from those used by other students is itself a form of discrimination. It's humiliating and degrading to be told that your very presence in a restroom is unacceptable.

For those of us who've never had to think about which restroom to use, it's tempting to dismiss the Trump administration's actions as insignificant. For transgender students, however, restroom use is anything but. Students who can't use the same restrooms as other boys and girls find themselves on the margins, literally and figuratively. They're forced to travel long distances to use other restrooms or hold it, risking painful urinary tract infections and dehydration. That's no way to learn. And these problems aren't limited to students. Transgender adults face the same struggles when trying to work, travel or simply go about their daily lives.

That's why a host of federal agencies, including the Department of Housing and Urban Development, the Department of Labor and the Equal Employment Opportunity Commission, concluded that transgender people should be allowed to use the restrooms that match the gender they live every day.

Putting the government's imprimatur on different and unequal treatment will do nothing but encourage bullying and harassment by other students. After all, children imitate.

The letter also falsely suggests that the departments need more time to take into account the experience of states and local school districts. But the experience of school administrators weighs in favor of inclusion, not against it. School districts across the country that have adopted inclusive policies have enjoyed a safer and more welcoming learning environment for all students, transgender and not.

Fortunately, the president and his executive agencies cannot change what Title IX says and means. Those jobs still belong to Congress and the federal courts. The Supreme Court is about to hear the case of Gavin Grimm, a 17-year-old whose Gloucester County, Va., school district barred him from using the boys' restrooms because he is transgender. Although Gavin used them — with permission from the school's principal — for weeks without incident, the school board adopted a policy excluding him from the boys' restrooms after some parents learned that a transgender boy was using them.

Gavin, then a sophomore in high school, displayed a hard-won maturity when he spoke at a school board hearing and pleaded, "All I want to do is be a normal child and use the restroom in peace." Unmoved, an adult in the community called Gavin a "freak" and compared him to a person who thinks he is a dog and wants to urinate on a fire hydrant.

A lower court has ruled in Gavin's favor, as have most courts to consider the question. Now the Supreme Court needs to solidify protections for Gavin and students like him across the country. Gavin's case could neutralize the Trump administration's cruel blow to vulnerable transgender youth. We have warned President Trump many times that we'll see him in court. This time, we're already there.

Supreme Court Won't Hear Major Case on Transgender Rights

BY ADAM LIPTAK | MARCH 6, 2017

WASHINGTON — Prompted by the Trump administration's reversal of the federal government's position on transgender rights, the Supreme Court announced on Monday that it would not decide whether a transgender boy in Virginia could use the boys' bathroom at his high school.

The decision not to take his case, which came as the court is awaiting the appointment of a ninth member, means there will be no ruling on the highly charged issue of transgender rights this term. The issue will almost certainly return to the Supreme Court, probably in a year or two.

Until then, lawsuits in the lower courts will proceed, the political climate and public opinion may shift, and the court's composition will almost certainly change.

Monday's development was a setback for transgender rights advocates, who had hoped the Supreme Court, which established a constitutional right to same-sex marriage two years ago, would aid their cause.

Instead, in a one-sentence order on Monday, the Supreme Court vacated an appeals court decision in favor of the student, Gavin Grimm, and sent the case back for further consideration in light of the new guidance from the administration.

The Supreme Court had agreed in October to hear the case, and the justices were scheduled to hear arguments this month. The case would have been the court's first encounter with transgender rights, and it would probably have been one of the biggest decisions of a fairly sleepy term.

"Thousands of transgender students across the country will have to wait even longer for a final decision from our nation's highest court affirming their basic rights," said Sarah Warbelow, the legal director of the Human Rights Campaign.

Kerri Kupec, a lawyer with Alliance Defending Freedom, a conservative Christian group, welcomed Monday's development.

"The first duty of school districts is to protect the bodily privacy rights of all of the students who attend their schools and to respect the rights of parents who understandably don't want their children exposed in intimate changing areas like locker rooms and showers," she said.

There are other cases on transgender rights in lower courts, including a challenge to a North Carolina law that, in government buildings, requires transgender people to use bathrooms that correspond with the gender listed on their birth certificates. The law has drawn protests, boycotts and lawsuits.

The question in the Virginia case was whether Mr. Grimm, 17, could use the boys' bathroom in his southeast Virginia high school. The Obama administration said yes, relying on its interpretation of a federal regulation under a 1972 law, Title IX, that bans discrimination "on the basis of sex" in schools that receive federal money.

The Department of Education said in 2015 that schools "generally must treat transgender students consistent with their gender identity." Last year, the department went further, saying that schools could lose federal money if they discriminated against transgender students.

The Trump administration withdrew that guidance last month, saying it had been formulated without "due regard for the primary role of the states and local school districts in establishing educational policy."

The letter announcing the new policy, signed by officials in the Education and Justice Departments, said schools must still take steps to protect all students from "discrimination, bullying or harassment."

Individual school districts remain free to let transgender students use the bathrooms of their choice. The practical effect of the Trump administration's change in position was limited, as a federal court had issued a nationwide injunction barring enforcement of the Obama administration's guidance.

AL DRAGO/THE NEW YORK TIMES

The Supreme Court vacated an appeals court decision in favor of a transgender boy, Gavin Grimm, and sent the case back for further consideration in light of new guidance from the Trump administration.

It will now be up to the United States Court of Appeals for the Fourth Circuit, in Richmond, Va., to answer whether Title IX protects the rights of Mr. Grimm and other transgender students.

Mr. Grimm attends Gloucester High School. For a time, school administrators allowed him to use the boys' bathroom, but the local school board later adopted a policy that required students to use the bathrooms and locker rooms for their "corresponding biological genders." The board added that "students with gender identity issues" would be allowed to use private bathrooms.

The American Civil Liberties Union, which represents Mr. Grimm, told the justices that requiring Mr. Grimm to use a private bathroom had been humiliating and had, quoting him, "turned him into 'a public spectacle' before the entire community, 'like a walking freak show.'"

After Mr. Grimm challenged the school board's bathroom policy in court in 2015, a divided Fourth Circuit panel ruled the policy unlawful. A trial judge then ordered school officials to let Mr. Grimm use the boys' bathroom.

A 1975 regulation adopted under Title IX allowed schools to provide "separate toilet, locker rooms and shower facilities on the basis of sex." The Fourth Circuit said that the rule was ambiguous and that the Education Department's interpretation of it was entitled to "controlling weight."

Both sides had hoped the Supreme Court would decide the case, Gloucester County School Board v. G.G., No. 16-273, even after the Trump administration withdrew its guidance on the meaning of the regulation.

In a letter to the justices last week, Joshua A. Block, a lawyer with the A.C.L.U., said the administration's change in position did not render the case moot, as the basic question of what Title IX meant remained. "The underlying principle that discrimination against transgender individuals is a form of discrimination on the basis of sex has been widely accepted in the lower courts for years," he wrote.

"Delaying resolution would provide no benefit to the court and would needlessly prolong harm to transgender students across the country awaiting this court's decision," Mr. Block wrote.

In a second letter, S. Kyle Duncan, a lawyer for the school board, agreed that the case should proceed, though he suggested a brief delay to allow the Trump administration to weigh in.

A ruling on the meaning of Title IX, Mr. Duncan wrote, "will save the parties — as well as public and private parties involved in similar disputes throughout the nation — enormous litigation costs as well as needless and divisive political controversy."

The Supreme Court rejected those requests, apparently preferring to wait for a cleaner presentation of the issues in a different case.

Gavin Grimm: The Fight for Transgender Rights Is Bigger Than Me

OPINION | BY GAVIN GRIMM | MARCH 7, 2017

JUST OVER TWO years ago, I started my sophomore year of high school. The summer before, I had come out to my family and friends as a transgender boy. I also came out to the school administration, telling them who I was and asking them to respect my gender identity. They assured me that teachers and administrators would call me Gavin, and use male pronouns when referring to me, and if anyone gave me any kind of trouble, it would be resolved right away. By the time I started school, I had legally changed my name and I was poised to start testosterone.

However, I was still anxious. I come from a fairly conservative community, and I wasn't sure that I'd be accepted for who I am. Because of this anxiety, I did not ask permission to use the boys' restroom. I was not yet accustomed to advocating for myself, and I worried that I would be asking for too much, too soon. Instead, I used the restroom in the nurse's office.

The office was far away from my classrooms that year. It took far too much time out of my day to use the restroom, especially when, in any class, I was just down the hall from a perfectly good boys' room. So I approached the administration again. This time, I asked to use the bathrooms that correspond to my gender identity. My principal told me the following day that I was free to use the boys' restrooms, and I did. For a period of roughly seven weeks, I went in and went out with no altercations of any kind. No physical or verbal confrontation. No restroom misconduct by or against me. This seven-week period showed me what it was like to be embraced by your school, and it gave me confidence that I would be able to live out a normal school year, unencumbered by restroom politics.

This was, unfortunately, a false sense of security. After that seven-week period, the school board held a meeting — a public conversation about my genitals and restroom usage — without notifying me first. My mother and I found out by chance less than 24 hours before the meeting was to happen. An old friend of my mother's had noticed a post going around Facebook, a rallying cry by adults in my community urging people to show up to the meeting in order to "keep that girl out of the boy's room."

I went to the meeting, in November 2014, and spoke at it. Family and a few friends stood by me, but nothing could have prepared that insecure 15 year old for what was to come. People speaking out against me made a point of referring to me with female honorifics and pronouns. They warned me that I was going to be raped or otherwise abused. They suggested that boys would sneak into the girls' room and harm their children. At a second meeting, a month later, the rhetoric was even more inflammatory. Word had spread throughout the community and people turned up in droves. After each frenzied remark, clapping and hollering reverberated throughout the room. I sat while people called me a freak. I sat while my community got together to banish a child from public life for the crime of harming no one. I sat while my school board voted to banish me to retrofitted broom closets or the nurse's restroom.

And then it was over. At least it felt like it, back then. I was back to being exiled. I heard sneers and whispers about me in the hallways. My school board had invalidated me in perhaps the most humiliating way possible.

But two years later — two crazy, stressful, busy, breathtaking, rewarding, beautiful, fantastic years later — I stand stronger and prouder than ever. I stand not only with my family and friends, but with millions of supporters who stand with me. I stand with so many wonderful people at the A.C.L.U. that I proudly call my family. I know now what I did not know then; I will be fine. Regardless of what obstacles come before me, regardless of what hatred or ignorance or discrimination I face, I will be fine, because I have love on my side.

This case will not be resolved until after I graduate. But this fight is bigger than me. I came to realize that very early on, and it is truer now than it ever has been. This fight is for other trans youth in my high school. It is for other trans youth in Virginia. It is for all trans youth who are in school or one day will be. It is for the friends and loved ones of these youth, who want these children to be happy and healthy, rather than at risk and in danger as so many trans people are.

I am often asked if I regret my actions, or if I would do anything differently if I had the chance. When people ask that, I immediately think about the hundreds of parents who have reached out to thank me on behalf of their children. I think of the hundreds of young people who have thanked me themselves. I think of the countless #StandWithGavin messages on social media, and the countless hugs and handshakes at school and on the sidewalks of my town. I think of people I've gotten to meet and grown to love. I think of how honored I am to carry the voice, in some way, of a community so rich and so colorful and so important. I think of how I've grown from that 15-year-old child, sitting in fear as he waits to hear what his future will be, into the young man who stands hand in hand with a huge community as we all prepare to take the next step in this fight. I think of my parents, unwavering and strong as pillars in my success and growth. And I say, "Absolutely not."

CHAPTER 4

Bathroom Laws in North Carolina and Texas

As Gavin Grimm's case was being fought in the courts, two other cases captured public attention. North Carolina passed HB-2, a controversial bill that spelled out which bathrooms transgender individuals should use. As a result, the Obama administration censured North Carolina, and major organizations, including the National Basketball Association, withdrew their support and affiliations from the state. Texas, meanwhile, debated a bathroom bill that would have enacted one of the most restrictive policies in the country.

North Carolina Bans Local Anti-Discrimination Policies

BY DAVE PHILIPPS | MARCH 23, 2016

NORTH CAROLINA LEGISLATORS, in a whirlwind special session on Wednesday, passed a wide-ranging bill barring transgender people from bathrooms and locker rooms that do not match the gender on their birth certificates.

Republicans unanimously supported the bill, while in the Senate, Democrats walked out in protest. "This is a direct affront to equality, civil rights and local autonomy," the Senate Democratic leader, Dan Blue, said in a statement.

North Carolina's governor, Pat McCrory, a Republican, signed the bill late Wednesday night.

The session, which was abruptly convened by Republican lawmakers on Tuesday, came in response to an antidiscrimination ordinance approved by the state's largest city, Charlotte, last month. That ordinance provided protections based on sexual orientation, gender expression and gender identity, including letting transgender people use the public bathrooms that correspond with their gender identity, not gender at birth.

The state bill, put together so quickly that many lawmakers had not seen it before it was introduced Wednesday morning, specifically bars people in North Carolina from using bathrooms that do not match their birth gender, and goes further to prohibit municipalities from creating their own antidiscrimination policies. Instead, it creates a statewide antidiscrimination policy — one that does not mention gay and transgender people. The bill also prohibits local governments from raising minimum wage levels above the state level — something a number of cities in other states have done.

Whether to allow transgender people access to bathrooms based on gender identity has touched off a national debate, and actions in recent weeks had appeared to turn in favor of that access. Earlier this month, South Dakota's Republican governor vetoed a bill banning access. A similar bill failed in Tennessee this week.

"North Carolina has gone against the trend," said Sarah Preston, the executive director for the North Carolina office of the American Civil Liberties Union. "And they crafted a bill that was more extreme than others. They specifically left gays, lesbians and the transgender community out of the antidiscrimination policy. They want to make it plain that they think that kind of discrimination is O.K."

Republicans stressed that the bill was passed not just to protect women and children from unwanted and potentially dangerous intrusions by biological males, but also to clarify legislative authority. On the House floor, Representative Dan Bishop, a Republican who sponsored the bill, described Charlotte's decision to enact an antidiscrimination measure as an "egregious overreach." With the state bill, he said, "What we are doing is preserving a sense of privacy people have long expected."

Some large firms in the state, many having policies that allow transgender access to bathrooms by identity, opposed the new bill. Dow Chemical, a major employer in the state, called the bill an "attempt to undermine equality."

In often emotional testimony on Wednesday before the bill was passed, those opposing transgender access described the issue as one of safety. Chloe Jefferson, a junior at Greenville Christian Academy, said letting biological males into women's bathrooms would expose girls to sexual predators, adding, "Girls like me should never be made to shower and undress in front of boys."

Madeleine Gause, a transgender woman who grew up in Hickory, where as a boy she was often bullied in the bathroom, told lawmakers that forcing transgender women to use the men's room posed its own risks. "I can't use the men's room. I won't go back. It is unsafe for me," she said. "And it freaks people out when I go to the men's room. Would you want to go to the men's room with me?"

She added that the fears of sexual predators were overblown.

"People aren't getting raped and murdered," she said. "They are just going to the bathroom."

Transgender Law Makes North Carolina Pioneer in Bigotry

BY THE NEW YORK TIMES | MARCH 25, 2016

OFFICIALS IN CHARLOTTE, N.C., spent more than a year carefully considering and debating an antidiscrimination ordinance that was passed in February to promote the city's culture of inclusiveness. State lawmakers quashed it on Wednesday by passing an appalling, unconstitutional bill that bars transgender people from using public restrooms that match their gender identity and prohibits cities from passing antidiscrimination ordinances that protect gay and transgender people.

Gov. Pat McCrory, who signed the bill into law late Wednesday, said it was necessary to undo Charlotte's ordinance, which included protections for gay and transgender people, because it allowed "men to use women's bathroom/locker room." Proponents of so-called bathroom bills, which have been introduced in state legislatures across the country, have peddled them by spuriously portraying transgender women as potential rapists. That threat exists only in the imagination of bigots. Supporters of the measures have been unable to point to a single case that justifies the need to legislate where people should be allowed to use the toilet. North Carolina is the first state to pass such a provision.

North Carolina lawmakers must have recognized that careful scrutiny of the bill would have doomed it. They convened a special session on Wednesday — which cost taxpayers $42,000 — to ram the bill through. The House allowed for 30 minutes of public debate, limiting speakers to two minutes. The Democrats walked out of the Senate in protest.

Inexplicably, lawmakers slipped a provision in the deceptively titled "Public Facilities Privacy & Security Act" that prohibits cities from setting a minimum wage higher than the state's, which is $7.25 per hour. That appears to be largely symbolic because local jurisdictions in North Carolina generally don't have the type of broad authority required to pass minimum wage requirements.

Under the law, people in North Carolina are required to use public restrooms that match the gender on their birth certificate. Transgender people in the state can request to have their birth certificate changed only if they have had gender reassignment surgery. Many transgender people cannot afford surgery or choose not to have it.

By promoting the ludicrous idea that transgender women are inherently dangerous, the law endangers citizens who are already disproportionately vulnerable to violence and stigmatization. Transgender men go largely unmentioned in bathroom bill debates, but that could change. James Parker Sheffield, a transgender man with a beard, exposed the foolishness of the law in a tweet to the governor. "It's now the law for me to share a restroom with your wife," he wrote, attaching a photo of himself.

North Carolina could face serious economic repercussions from the law. It can expect a backlash from leading employers, a potential cut in federal education funding and lawsuits challenging the constitutionality of the law. American Airlines, which has a hub in Charlotte, and PayPal, which recently announced it would create 400 jobs in the state, are among several companies that have already criticized the law.

Mr. McCrory, who is running for re-election, may have assumed the bill would help him in a tight race against Attorney General Roy Cooper, a Democrat who called the measure shameful. "Not only does this hurt North Carolina families, but it hurts our economy as well," Mr. Cooper said in a video message. Voters should reject the candidate who made the state a pioneer in bigotry.

U.S. Warns North Carolina That Transgender Bill Violates Civil Rights Laws

BY ERIC LICHTBLAU AND RICHARD FAUSSET | MAY 4, 2016

WASHINGTON — The Justice Department warned the State of North Carolina on Wednesday that its new law limiting bathroom access violated the civil rights of transgender people, a finding that could mean millions of dollars in lost federal funds.

In a letter to Gov. Pat McCrory, Vanita Gupta, the top civil rights lawyer for the Justice Department, said that "both you and the State of North Carolina" were in violation of civil rights law, and gave him until Monday to decide "whether you will remedy these violations."

A Justice Department official said that federal officials hoped that the state would agree to comply voluntarily with federal civil rights law by abandoning the measure. But the department has a number of tools it can use to try to force compliance, including denying federal funds or asking a court to do so, said the official, who spoke on condition of anonymity.

The ultimatum escalated a contentious national debate over North Carolina's new legal stance on transgender and gay people, and set up what could be a lengthy showdown between the state and the Obama administration.

In a statement, Mr. McCrory, a Republican, said: "The right and expectation of privacy in one of the most private areas of our personal lives is now in jeopardy. We will be reviewing to determine the next steps."

Phil Berger, the president pro tempore of the State Senate, accused the Justice Department of "a gross overreach" that he said "deserves to be struck down in federal court." Tim Moore, the speaker of the House, called the letter an attempt to "circumvent the will of the electorate and instead unilaterally exert its extreme agenda."

The state measure, House Bill 2, known as HB2, was signed into law in March and says the bathroom a person uses is determined by his or her biological gender at birth. That requirement "is facially discriminatory against transgender employees" because it treats them differently from other employees, Ms. Gupta wrote.

As a result, "we have concluded that in violation of Title VII, the state is engaged in a pattern or practice of resistance to the full enjoyment of Title VII right by employees of public agencies," she said. The letter was first reported by The Charlotte Observer.

The law has become an issue in the presidential campaign and has prompted boycotts of North Carolina from celebrities like Bruce Springsteen, as well as calls for repeal by a number of businesses, some of which have canceled plans to create new jobs in the state.

Opponents cheered the Justice Department's move.

"I think it makes clear what we've known all along, which is that HB2 is deeply discriminatory and violates civil rights law in all kinds of manners," said State Representative Chris Sgro of Greensboro.

Matt McTighe, executive director of Freedom for All Americans, an L.G.B.T. rights group, said in a statement Wednesday that "actions have consequences, and Governor McCrory and his legislative allies are now paying the price for this anti-transgender law that they so hurriedly enacted.

"HB2 is a solution in a search of a problem that simply doesn't exist, and lawmakers must take immediate action to fully repeal it," he said. "The state's economy and reputation have suffered enough, and now students all across the state stand to lose out on nearly $1 billion in critical funding because of HB2. The livelihoods of North Carolina's families are at stake, and there is no excuse for inaction."

In December 2014, the attorney general at the time, Eric H. Holder Jr., directed the Justice Department to begin including gender identity —

including transgender status — as a basis for discrimination claims under federal civil rights law.

That decision reversed a policy at the Justice Department that specifically excluded transgender people from federal protection. Mr. Holder called the decision "an important shift," meant to affirm the Justice Department's commitment "to protecting the civil rights of all Americans."

In addition, the Equal Opportunity Employment Commission held last year that "equal access to restrooms is a significant, basic condition of employment" and that denying access to transgender individuals was discriminatory, Ms. Gupta noted, in her letter to Mr. McCrory.

The Justice Department's threat was not the only front opened Wednesday in the battle over transgender bathroom rights.

In Illinois, a group calling itself Students and Parents for Privacy filed a lawsuit against the Department of Education, the Justice Department, Attorney General Loretta E. Lynch and the school directors of Township High School District 211 in Cook County, Ill., seeking to stop the district from "forcing 14- to 17-year-old girls to use locker rooms and restrooms with biological males."

In November, federal education authorities ruled that the school district, near Chicago, violated Title IX, the federal law that forbids discrimination on the basis of sex in public education, when it did not allow a transgender student who said she identifies as a girl to change and shower in the girls' locker room without restrictions.

The fact that the student, who is biologically male, now uses the bathroom and locker rooms at William Fremd High School, the lawsuit states, creates an "intimidating and hostile environment" for girls, according to the lawsuit, which was filed Wednesday in the United States District Court in the Northern District of Illinois.

The suit also asks the court to set aside a Department of Education rule in which transgender students are covered under Title IX.

Meanwhile, in Oxford, Ala., the City Council on Wednesday rescinded an ordinance it had passed the week before that forbade people to use a public restroom that did not match their gender at birth, according to the Alabama news website al.com.

The news service reported that at least one of the three members who voted to rescind the ordinance in the 3-2 vote was influenced by a city attorney's opinion that the ordinance might be illegal under Title IX.

ERIC LICHTBLAU REPORTED FROM WASHINGTON, AND RICHARD FAUSSET FROM ATLANTA. ALAN BLINDER CONTRIBUTED REPORTING FROM ATLANTA.

N.B.A. to Move All-Star Game from North Carolina

BY SCOTT CACCIOLA AND ALAN BLINDER | JULY 21, 2016

THE NATIONAL BASKETBALL ASSOCIATION on Thursday dealt a blow to the economy and prestige of North Carolina by pulling next February's All-Star Game from Charlotte to protest a state law that eliminated anti-discrimination protections for lesbian, gay, bisexual and transgender people.

The move was among the most prominent consequences since the law, which also bars transgender people from using bathrooms in public buildings that do not correspond with their birth gender, was passed in March.

The league, which has become increasingly involved in social issues, said that both it and the Hornets, the N.B.A. team based in Charlotte, had been talking to state officials about changing the law but that time had run out because of the long lead time needed to stage the game. The N.B.A. said it hoped the game could be played in Charlotte in 2019, with the clear implication that the law would have to be changed before then.

"While we recognize that the N.B.A. cannot choose the law in every city, state and country in which we do business, we do not believe we can successfully host our All-Star festivities in Charlotte in the climate created by the current law," a statement by the league said.

Gov. Pat McCrory of North Carolina issued a blistering statement soon after the announcement by the N.B.A. He said "the sports and entertainment elite," among others, had "misrepresented our laws and maligned the people of North Carolina simply because most people believe boys and girls should be able to use school bathrooms, locker rooms and showers without the opposite sex present."

Mr. McCrory did not specifically refer to the N.B.A. in his statement, but he said that "American families should be on notice that the selective corporate elite are imposing their political will on communities in which they do business, thus bypassing the democratic and legal process."

Others weighed in in support of the N.B.A.'s move, including two of its broadcast partners — Turner Sports and ESPN.

In taking the action it did, the N.B.A. is following the path already taken by others. A number of musicians, including Bruce Springsteen, Ringo Starr and Itzhak Perlman, canceled concerts in North Carolina to protest the law, and there have been calls for repeal of the legislation by a number of businesses, some of which have canceled plans to create new jobs in the state.

All-Star weekend is one of the flashiest and most lucrative events on the league's annual schedule. In addition to the game, the league arranges three days full of activities for fans. There is a separate game for the league's rising stars, a dunk contest and a 3-point contest.

Now all of that will be held elsewhere next February, with the N.B.A. to announce a new site for the game in the next few weeks.

The decision by the N.B.A. comes after its commissioner, Adam Silver, had strongly hinted that such a move might be coming and again thrusts the league into the middle of social issues now gripping the nation, setting the league apart, at least for now, from Major League Baseball, the National Football League and other sports entities.

In recent weeks, a number of the N.B.A.'s top players have spoken out in dismay as they reacted to shootings around the country that have left police officers dead in two cities and the police accused of deadly recklessness in several other cases.

And last December, the N.B.A. participated in a series of television advertisements denouncing gun violence that aired during its long Christmas Day schedule of games.

Players in the N.B.A.'s sister league — the W.N.B.A. — have also become vocal. In recent weeks, players on several W.N.B.A. teams wore T-shirts during warm-ups before games that addressed the recent shootings.

On Thursday, just hours before the N.B.A. announced it was pulling the All-Star Game out of Charlotte, the W.N.B.A. fined the players on three teams $500 apiece, and the clubs $5,000, saying it had no problem with the players' public "engagement" with difficult social issues but drew the line at violating the guidelines on team uniforms.

A number of W.N.B.A. players stated their unhappiness with the fines and they drew support from the Knicks' Carmelo Anthony, who has been one of the most outspoken N.B.A. players this past month. He said Thursday that he saw no reason for "anybody to get fined."

The action by the N.B.A. is also certain to inject new fervor into the debate about North Carolina's law, which many people still refer to as House Bill 2.

Before its adjournment this month, and in defiance of pleas from public officials and corporate executives in Charlotte, the General Assembly resisted demands that it back away from some of the most contentious elements of the law, which supporters have argued is about public safety, not discrimination.

The fate of the law, which the United States Justice Department has challenged as a violation of the Civil Rights Act of 1964, will most likely be settled in court. A federal judge in Winston-Salem, N.C., will hear arguments next month about whether to block the law while the litigation is pending.

Even before the N.B.A.'s action on Thursday, Republicans in North Carolina had signaled repeatedly that the league's misgivings about the law were unlikely to persuade its supporters.

"Our values are not shaped by the N.B.A. or Bruce Springsteen or some opinion poll," state Representative Phil Shepard, a Republican and a Baptist minister, declared at a rally in April. "We're standing strong."

But it was also in April that Mr. Silver was spelling out how problematic the N.B.A. thought the law was. He noted at the time that the league had a "long record of speaking out where we see discrimination."

Last week, Mr. Silver weighed in again, saying of North Carolina's legislators: "We were frankly hoping that they would make some steps toward modifying the legislation and frankly I was disappointed that they didn't."

It remains to be seen whether any other major sports organization may take action in connection with the North Carolina law. Notably, the N.C.A.A.'s Division I men's basketball tournament has first- and second-round games scheduled for North Carolina in 2017 and 2018, but has given no indication that it might move them elsewhere.

However, Mike Krzyzewski, the coach at Duke, which is in Durham, N.C., and has long been one of the N.C.A.A.'s most prominent basketball teams, has been sharply critical of the North Carolina law.

He has been in Las Vegas this week coaching the men's national basketball team as it trains for next month's Summer Olympics, and Thursday he said North Carolina had "lost a lot" because of the legislation.

He had previously described the law as "embarrassing."

Chris Sgro, the executive director of Equality North Carolina and the only openly gay member of the state's General Assembly, said in a telephone interview Thursday that the N.B.A. was making a strong statement by removing one of its marquee events from Charlotte.

"The state of North Carolina grossly overreached by passing the worst anti-L.G.B.T. bill in the nation, and they have cost us the N.B.A. All-Star Game," Mr. Sgro said. "The blame for $100 million in economic loss and the impact that it has on the city of Charlotte and the entire state is squarely at the feet of the McCrory machine."

State legislators are not scheduled to reconvene until January.

"I could very well see a special session to deal with this issue," Mr. Sgro said. "We're going to continue to sustain incredible economic harm if we don't repeal House Bill 2."

Texas Bathroom Bill Has Emotions, and Stakes, Running High

BY MANNY FERNANDEZ AND DAVID MONTGOMERY | JULY 21, 2017

AUSTIN, TEX. — Amid conflicting pressures from gay rights groups, social conservatives, corporations and the state's Republican leadership, the Texas Senate on Friday waded back into the volatile issue of restricting bathroom use by transgender people in government buildings and schools.

The issue, which roiled North Carolina for more than a year and led to boycotts and other economic blowback, has become one of the most heated and high-stakes political dramas in Texas. It has deepened the divide between moderate Republicans and social conservatives and caused widespread fears that a wave of boycotts and protests would do serious damage to the Texas economy, which is still feeling the effects of a drop in the price of oil.

Given the presence in Texas, the second most populous state, of three of the nation's 10 largest cities, the economic stakes from boycotts or cancellations of concerts and athletic events could dwarf what played out in North Carolina.

The so-called bathroom bill was approved by a Republican-dominated Senate committee on Friday evening and now heads to the full Senate for a vote, part of a fast-paced push by social conservatives to try to pass the measure into law in the coming weeks.

Earlier on Friday, more than 250 supporters and opponents of the bill signed up to testify before the Senate Committee on State Affairs. The testimony began in the morning and continued into the evening. The hearing centered on two bills requiring transgender people to use the bathroom, locker room or shower that corresponds with the sex on their birth certificate, as opposed to their gender identity, in public buildings, including schools. The version that the committee ultimately approved passed by a vote of 8 to 1.

The newly elected mayor of San Antonio, Ron Nirenberg, told the senators in opposing the bill that the mere filing of it has already cost his city millions of dollars in lost conventions. A number of transgender Texans testified against it, including Sierra Jane Davis, 22, a transgender woman from Austin and a former Marine.

Ms. Davis, who has the Marine Corps emblem tattooed on her left arm, said in an interview outside the hearing that the bill would "open the floodgates to more and more legislation, and lets the public see that we are allowed to be discriminated against."

Alisa Miller, an Austin resident who is the mother of a 15-year-old transgender girl, prepared to testify wearing a gray T-shirt reading, "Don't Discriminate in the Lone Star State." Her daughter, Maeve, who transitioned to a girl when she was 14, now uses the girls' room at her Austin high school and worries about being bullied if she is forced to use a boys' room.

"She's very concerned," Ms. Miller said. "It's potentially not a safe situation for her."

Social conservatives, led by Lt. Gov. Dan Patrick, have denied that the bill discriminates against anyone and have accused critics of exaggerating the potential economic damage. They said the issue is about public safety and women's privacy.

"It's not about transgender," Trayce Bradford, the president of a conservative group called the Texas Eagle Forum, told the Senate committee. "It's about feeling safe. There has to be some boundaries."

Ms. Bradford, who said she was stalked and sexually assaulted in college, said conservative activists have been unfairly accused of spreading hate by backing the legislation. "I don't know of any conservative who wants to serve as the potty police," she said.

Terry Holcomb, a leader of the Republican Party of Texas who testified in support of the bill, described it as a common-sense issue that has been "deliberately misconstrued and mischaracterized." Charles Flowers, the senior pastor of Faith Outreach Center International in San Antonio, who was planning to testify but ultimately did not, said he and other ministers have urged their congregations to tell lawmakers to vote in favor of the bill, which he said would leave women and girls "at risk" without its protections.

"It's not a Democratic or Republican issue," Mr. Flowers said.

On Sunday, IBM took out full-page ads in major Texas newspapers, saying that the company "firmly opposes" any measure that would harm the state's gay, lesbian and transgender community and make it harder for businesses to recruit and retain talent.

The next day, the chief executives of 14 Dallas-based companies — including corporate giants like American Airlines, AT&T Inc., Southwest Airlines and Texas Instruments — sent a letter to the governor expressing concern that the bill "would seriously hurt the state's ability to attract new businesses, investment and jobs."

And on Wednesday, the presiding officers of the Episcopal Church wrote to the speaker of the Texas House and suggested that if the bill passed, the church would cancel its nine-day General Convention in Austin scheduled for July 2018.

"In 1955, we were forced to move a General Convention from Houston to another state because Texas laws prohibited black and white Episcopalians from being treated equally," read the letter from Bishop Michael B. Curry and another leader. "We would not stand then for Episcopalians to be discriminated against, and we cannot countenance it now."

Jeff Moseley, chief executive of the Texas Association of Business, the state's most influential business lobby, announced that the group was taking its opposition to the bill to the airwaves by making a "seven-figure media buy." The group has long aligned itself with the state's conservative causes and issues, and has rarely taken public stands on social issues.

"The bathroom bill distracts from the real challenges we face and would result in terrible economic consequences — on talent, on tourism, on investment, on growth, and on small businesses," Mr. Moseley said in a statement.

The Legislature failed to pass a bathroom bill during the regular legislative session that ended in May, with moderate Republicans in the House clashing with social conservatives in the Senate. Several Republicans in the House, led by Joe Straus, the speaker, worry that a North Carolina-style series of boycotts, canceled conventions and negative national attention would hit Texas if the bill passed.

The lieutenant governor, Mr. Patrick, who has been the driving force behind the bill, effectively forced Gov. Greg Abbott to call lawmakers back for a 30-day special session to give the bathroom bill another shot at passage. Mr. Patrick used legislation that was vital to keeping a few government agencies operating as a tool to get Mr. Abbott to order lawmakers back to Austin.

The bathroom bill was expected to easily win approval in the Senate during the special session, which began on Tuesday, but its chances are less assured in the House, and it was unclear whether moderate Republicans will be successful in stalling, killing or watering down the bill.

The measure was filed by State Senator Lois W. Kolkhorst, a Republican, and requires all multiple-occupancy restrooms, showers and locker rooms in public buildings to be designated for and used only by "persons of the same sex as stated on a person's birth certificate." The bill applies to multiple-occupancy restrooms in local government buildings and public schools.

It also prohibits localities and schools from adopting anti-discrimination policies that allow transgender people to use the bathroom that corresponds with their gender identity.

Texas Transgender Bathroom Bill Falters Amid Mounting Opposition

BY DAVID MONTGOMERY | AUG. 8, 2017

AUSTIN, TEX. — With little more than a week left in Texas' 30-day special legislative session, a barrage of corporate advertising and activism has the potential to sink legislation restricting transgender bathroom use that has been a flash point in the state's culture wars.

Social conservatives and the state's powerful lieutenant governor, Dan Patrick, have backed the legislation. Gay rights groups, business groups and the House speaker, Joe Straus, one of the few powerful moderate voices in the Texas Legislature, have opposed it. But after the State Senate, where Mr. Patrick presides, passed a bill, a narrower one is showing few signs of life in the 150-member House.

The effort is now focused on the House version, but State Representative Jonathan Stickland, one of the bill's 46 co-authors and a member of the Tea Party-backed Freedom Caucus, said he was pessimistic about its chances of being allowed to advance to a vote.

"I think the Straus team has already decided that they are not going to let it out," said Mr. Stickland, who, like other members of the staunchly conservative caucus, persistently defies the speaker's leadership. "This is clearly part of a national agenda that is being pushed by the progressive left, and I think that that is just all coming to a head here."

The Senate bill would require transgender people to use bathrooms in schools and local government buildings corresponding to the gender listed on their birth certificates or state-issued identification cards. The House bill would prevent school districts and county or local governments from adopting or enforcing nondiscrimination ordinances that would allow transgender people to use bathrooms of their choice. The ordinance override provision is also an element in the Senate bill.

Although law enforcement, religious groups and transgender advocates have all been part of the opposing coalition, big business has been a dominant force throughout the debate.

"Corporate America is stepping forward, speaking loudly about the fact that this will have a chilling effect on business opportunity in this state," said State Representative Byron Cook, a Republican and the chairman of the House State Affairs Committee, who has thus far refused to call a hearing on the bill. "I'm hearing from many major corporations about this bill and the effect it will have."

Corporations active in Texas that have opposed the measure include IBM, Amazon, Apple, Dell, Microsoft, Intel, Capital One, Ben & Jerry's, Facebook, American Airlines, Southwest Airlines and United Airlines.

More than 650 businesses, chambers of commerce, and convention and visitors' bureaus have come out against the bill, according to the Texas Association of Business, which is leading the charge to defeat the legislation. The list includes 50 Fortune 500 companies and more than 400 small businesses, according to the group.

The association is the most powerful business lobby in the state, representing companies with more than two million employees and $8 billion in business. The group's president, Chris Wallace, said the association moved quickly to form a coalition, Keep Texas Open for Business, against legislation when it became apparent that the bathroom battle was heading to Texas.

"We do not want to do anything to tarnish Texas' brand," he said.

The strategy has included a seven-figure radio ad buy, strategically targeted letters signed by prominent chief executives, lobbying blitzes throughout the Capitol and rallies on the Capitol grounds.

Several dozen women, predominately business owners and executives, many accompanied by their children, gathered on the south steps of the state Capitol on Tuesday as 15 speakers attacked the legislation as the work of "extremist" politicians that will blunt the economy and foster discrimination and hate crimes.

"I don't want my child to be a statistic of the 2017 special session," said Kimberly Shappley, a registered nurse and ordained minister from the Houston suburbs who was accompanied by her 6-year-old transgender daughter, Kai.

Business executives repeatedly cite North Carolina as Exhibit A in opposing the bill, pointing to millions of dollars in economic losses through boycotts and the cancellations of sports events and concerts after a similar bill passed there in 2016. A study commissioned by the business association also projects billions of dollars in losses in Texas.

Mr. Patrick and other supporters of the legislation say the projections in Texas and the impact in North Carolina have been vastly exaggerated.

IBM, which has 10,000 employees in Texas, has been at the forefront of the drive to kill the legislation. The corporation placed a full-page ad against the measure in major Texas newspapers the day before the session started and has staged two "fly-ins" of company executives to appeal to lawmakers. Virginia M. Rometty, the company's chief executive, has spoken with Gov. Greg Abbott and Mr. Straus on the phone to air the company's concerns.

Business's involvement has increasingly become a target for proponents as they accelerate their efforts in the remaining days of the session.

"I don't think anybody has seen corporations engage on an issue like this outside the framework of taxes and regulations in our memory," said Dave Welch of the Texas Pastor Council, which is a leading supporter of the legislation. "I think it's a combination of a rising moral bankruptcy in corporate America, in which the only thing they support is their image and their bottom line."

A video ad campaign titled "Big Business Hypocrisy," sponsored by Family Research Council Action, says major corporations, hotels and airlines are demanding that "Texas expose women and children to policies that could endanger them in the most private of places" — the bathroom — while refusing to "enact the same unsafe policies in their own facilities."

If the session goes all 30 days — and it could end earlier — lawmakers would adjourn on Aug 16. Mr. Abbott, a Republican, has given no hints on whether he would call another session, although he has been particularly insistent that lawmakers give Texans new safeguards against rising property taxes.

As for the bathroom legislation, the governor told the Austin American-Statesman newspaper on Friday that it was "way premature" to conclude that the House bill wouldn't come up for a vote.

The intensity of the debate has raised questions about the future relationship between business groups and the state's Republican leadership, which have shared a decades-long bond. Mr. Wallace, president of the Texas business association, said the bond would remain unbroken despite the differences in the current showdown.

"Ninety-plus percent of the time we are in agreement," he said. "We just happen to disagree on this issue."

The Foolish Transgender Debate in Texas

OPINION | BY THE NEW YORK TIMES | AUG. 11, 2017

WHILE MUCH OF THE NATION appears to be adjusting to the transgender rights movement, social conservatives in the Texas Legislature — prodded by Lt. Gov. Dan Patrick, a Republican — continue their obsessive campaign to restrict the bathroom rights of transgender citizens.

They are fighting to the very end of the current special session, in the face of a storm of powerful opposition that ranges from the state's Fortune 500 companies and business leaders to police chiefs, sports and tourism executives, concerned parents and pastors in an evangelical community divided over the lack of basic charity underlying the anti-transgender legislation.

Even so, the State Senate passed Mr. Patrick's restrictive measure last month mandating that transgender Texans use only those public bathrooms that match the sex on their birth certificates, not those matching the gender with which they identify. The measure also blocks moves by many sympathetic local governments to pass nondiscrimination laws that guarantee transgender people the right to use the bathrooms of their choice.

In the vote, the Senate chose to ignore the ignominious fate of North Carolina legislators who had to retreat from similar narrow-minded restrictions this year in the face of a revolt by business and community leaders and a boycott by influential institutions that cost the state hundreds of millions of dollars in revenue and business profits. Texas senators also ignored the practical question of how this mandate would ever be enforced, considering the factors of privacy and documentation at stake.

Of such is Texas politics. "It's bad political theater," Police Chief Art Acevedo of Houston neatly summarized the debate. "And at the end of the day, it is bad for Texas," he said, emphasizing to lawmakers that there was no crisis of transgender people preying on the innocent in bathrooms.

The chief's view may be endorsed by many Texans, yet a final fight is underway in the House, where the speaker, Joe Straus, a moderate Republican, sounds determined to stop the social conservatives' drive and kill the measure. In the quirky, unpredictable ways of Texas politics, however, the Republican governor, Greg Abbott, cautions it is "way premature" to say there will be no vote.

Politicians have played this issue for conservative support, just as President Trump did in suddenly announcing a ban on transgender people serving in the armed forces. A reluctant Pentagon has so far shown no sign that it will follow through on the commander in chief's decision.

Defeat of the Texas legislation would provide a bright exclamation point for the progress of the transgender rights movement. As it stands, the debate is already a rousing success for drawing out the mass of corporate and social forces that want no part of making Texas a citadel of cruel discrimination.

CHAPTER 5

Transgender in the Military

After years of debate, transgender individuals won a victory in 2016 when Ashton B. Carter, the Secretary of Defense, declared that transgender men and women would be able to serve openly in the military. This came as a victory for transgender individuals in uniform, who had been serving in the armed forces for decades without medical and institutional protection. In 2017, Trump announced that he was revoking the policy, reigniting the debate over transgender service members and sending the lives of transgender troops into chaos.

The Courage of Transgender Soldiers

BY JULIA BAIRD | FEB. 21, 2014

SYDNEY, AUSTRALIA — It was 2 a.m., just a few days before Christmas, in a remote part of Afghanistan. Eight hours into a 16-hour shift, Ryan, a 23-year-old American naval sailor, was standing tense and alert, watching the footage of soldiers undertaking a nearby mission on a screen in front of him.

Suddenly, a hand clapped onto his back. Wheeling around to look at the face of his senior officer, Ryan knew the moment he had feared had come: His superiors had found out that his enlisted paperwork described him as female. Within three hours, he was on a plane.

Ryan, who is now stationed on a base in the United States awaiting a potential discharge, recently described that day to me. Ryan is the name his mother would have given him if he had been identified as male at birth. He does not want to reveal his real name because his case is being processed by the military.

While the repeal of "don't ask, don't tell" in 2011 meant gays and lesbians could serve openly in the American military, transgender people still cannot, because the military defines gender nonconformity as a psychological disorder. So transgender soldiers serve in silence, facing dismissal if exposed.

This isn't the case in other countries. At least 12 now officially allow transgender individuals to serve openly in their defense forces. Britain has allowed transgender people to serve openly since 1999, and Australia since 2010.

The flags of these countries had hung above Ryan's control station in Afghanistan. "I wear an American uniform and I represent a country supposedly defined by liberty and equality," he told me. But "my allies are welcome to serve in a way that has most certainly just cost me my livelihood. If these countries' soldiers, sailors, airmen and marines can serve openly and authentically as transgender women and men, why can't I?"

Nine percent of transgender people who have served in the American military report being discharged because of being transgender or gender nonconforming. Almost all of the rest stay quiet for fear of harassment or abuse.

A Harvard study published last year found that most transgender military personnel in America are white, educated and middle-aged. And most eventually transitioned from male to female. It also found that 20 percent of transgender people had served in the military — double the rate of the general population. (There is a theory that many seek "hypermasculine" experiences to suppress their desire to be female.) A University of California survey found almost all — 97 percent — were not able to transition until after they left the service.

But there's a shift happening. According to data from the Department of Veterans Affairs, the number of veterans seeking advice on transgender issues has doubled in the past 10 years. And hundreds of currently serving transgender members of the armed forces have joined an underground support movement called SPART*A. (About 20 of them are out to their peers, and a handful are also out to their superiors. They describe meeting with wildly varying degrees of support, much as gays and lesbians found before the repeal of "don't ask, don't tell.")

Transgender men and women are not banned from serving by congressional law, but by military medical codes. These codes classify being transgender as a psychological disorder, which was in line with the Diagnostic and Statistical Manual of Mental Disorders III, published in 1980. But the latest edition of the manual, the D.S.M.-5, released last May, replaced "Gender Identity Disorder" with "gender dysphoria." The point of the change, according to the American Psychiatric Association, was to make it clear that "gender nonconformity is not in itself a mental disorder."

The military has not acknowledged this shift. Asked if the Defense Department would reconsider its policies and make the necessary regulatory change, a spokesman for the Pentagon, Lt. Cmdr. Nate Christensen, responded, "Department of Defense regulations don't allow transgender individuals to serve in the U.S. military, based upon medical standards for military service."

So the global anomalies remain. And a growing number are asking why.

A new documentary series called "TransMilitary," which is scheduled to be released online in the fall, will contrast the experiences of transgender people in the armed forces in America and Britain. Fiona Dawson, the show's host and producer, says the difference between the countries is "shocking." While she has found several transgender members of the armed forces under investigation in America with likely discharge, in Britain, she found support, and some celebration.

"A captain in the British Army even had a 'patch party' thrown for her to celebrate her first day of hormones," she told me. "Her colleagues slapped Band-Aids on their arms while she applied her first hormone patch. These are the human interactions that build a trusting, cohesive and robust team."

Across the world, bold transgender men and women are stepping into the public light to show it is possible to live authentic lives while serving their countries. Many face rejection, many struggle with suicidal thoughts, and the great majority serve in secret. But others are speaking out.

Allyson Robinson, now an L.G.B.T. consultant, served in the United States Army and was ordained as a Baptist minister before coming out as transgender and transitioning to female. She says her greatest struggle when studying at West Point was the honor code — "a cadet will not lie, cheat, steal or tolerate those who do." Having to conceal her true gender identity felt like a violation of that code.

But since transitioning, she says she has experienced "nothing but respect" from people in the military. Once, when she told a puzzled cadet at the West Point gate that she had studied there, he clicked his heels and said: "Well, then, welcome home, ma'am." She cried all the way to the parking lot, and cries when retelling the story now.

One of the highest-ranking transgender military officers in the world — if not the highest — is Lt. Col. Cate McGregor of the Australian Defense Force. When she decided to undergo gender reassignment in 2012, she offered to resign. But her boss, the chief of Army, Lt. Gen. David Morrison, refused to allow it. She is now a prominent and widely respected officer (and cricket commentator) who attributes her acceptance to her colleagues' support and Australia's "live and let live" pragmatism. Most "alpha Aussie blokes," she says, were content that she was "still into chicks" and could still hit a cricket ball, which amused her: "There is a groping towards a paradigm of blokeyness they can accept." Every day now, she says, living as a woman, "it feels amazing to be alive."

General Morrison said that watching Colonel McGregor's struggles has deepened his understanding of what it means to be transgender:

"My hat goes off to everyone who does it because they are trying to be true to themselves. It takes an enormous amount of courage. And if an army can't respect courage, then there's something wrong."

Courage, surely, should be part of any honor code, too.

Transgender People Will Be Allowed to Serve Openly in Military

BY MATTHEW ROSENBERG | JUNE 30, 2016

WASHINGTON — Defense Secretary Ashton B. Carter on Thursday removed one of the final barriers to military service by lifting the Pentagon's ban on transgender people serving openly in the armed forces.

"Effective immediately, transgender Americans may serve openly," Mr. Carter said. "They can no longer be discharged or otherwise separated from the military just for being transgender."

The decision pushes forward a transformation of the military that Mr. Carter has accelerated in the last year with the opening of all combat roles to women and the appointment of the first openly gay Army secretary. He made his feelings on ending the transgender ban clear last year, when he called it outdated and ordered officials across the military to begin examining what would need to be done to lift it.

When Mr. Carter ordered that assessment, there were already thousands of transgender people in the military. But until Thursday, most had been forced into an existence shrouded in secrecy to avoid being discharged, a situation much like that faced by gay men, lesbians and bisexuals before the lifting of the "don't ask, don't tell" policy in 2011.

Transgender people have "deployed all over the world, serving on aircraft, submarines, forward operating bases and right here in the Pentagon," Mr. Carter told reporters. "The lack of clear guidelines for how to handle this issue puts the commanders and the service members in a difficult and unfair position."

For many transgender people, the lack of clarity described by Mr. Carter has resulted in them being forced out of uniform. Army Capt. Sage Fox, 43, was in the reserves when she told her unit that she was transgender in November 2013. A month later, she was placed on inactive status and has not done any reserve duty since.

She called the end of the ban "thrilling news," and said she expected to be reactivated as a reservist in the coming weeks. She was confident that the military would adapt.

"We're military officers. We are trained to be adaptable, and I get so frustrated when people think we're not going to be able to deal with this," she said in an interview. "You're on the battlefield, the situation changes in the blink of an eye, we adapt and overcome. That's what we do."

Mr. Carter said the Pentagon would cover the medical costs of those in uniform who are seeking to undergo gender transition, though it would expect new recruits who are transgender to spend at least 18 months in their transitioned gender identity before joining the military.

The Pentagon also plans to begin a broad, yearlong training program about the changes for service members up and down the ranks.

The military's top leaders, including Gen. Joseph F. Dunford Jr., the chairman of the Joint Chiefs of Staff, were on board with ending the prohibition, Mr. Carter said, although none of the military's top brass appeared with him for the announcement.

Lifting the ban on transgender people has faced resistance from some at the highest ranks of the military, who have expressed concerns over what they consider to be a social experiment that could potentially harm the military's readiness and effectiveness in combat.

When Mr. Carter in July 2015 first ordered the military to begin examining how to lift the ban, he indicated the work would be completed earlier this year. But as winter turned to spring and the ban remained in place, "I think everyone was raising questions about what was going to happen," said Aaron Belkin, the director of the Palm Center, a research institute that has studied the effects of having gays, lesbians and transgender people in the military.

Still, the announcement on Thursday came faster than Mr. Belkin would have predicted when he began to press for lifting the transgender ban three years ago, after the end of "don't ask, don't tell."

"I thought it would take 10 or 15 years" he said.

Mr. Belkin said that the end of "don't ask, don't tell," the opening of combat roles to women and the lifting of the ban on transgender people were "all about the same idea — that job assignments should be based on merit, not about gender identity or sexuality."

Those within the military who did not feel similarly were unsurprisingly silent on Thursday. Republicans in Congress were not.

Senator Jim Inhofe of Oklahoma, a Republican member of the Senate Armed Services Committee, called for the new policy to not be carried out until Congress could convene hearings. And Representative Mac Thornberry of Texas, the chairman of the House Armed Services Committee, released a statement saying he would examine "legislative options to address the readiness issues associated with this new policy."

"Our military readiness — and hence our national security — is dependent on our troops' being medically ready and deployable," Mr. Thornberry said. "The administration seems unwilling or unable to assure the Congress and the American people that transgender individuals will meet these individual readiness requirements at a time when our armed forces are deployed around the world."

But several studies on the issue have concluded that lifting the ban is unlikely to have any appreciable effect on the readiness of the armed forces.

Estimates of the number of transgender service members have varied, but the number most often cited comes from a study by the RAND Corporation and commissioned by Mr. Carter. It found that out of the approximately 1.3 million active-duty service members, an estimated 2,450 were transgender, and that every year, about 65 service members would seek to make a gender transition.

Providing medical care to those seeking to transition would cost $2.9 million to $4.2 million a year for the Pentagon, which spends about $6 billion of its $610 billion annual budget on medical costs for active-duty service members, according to the report, which was completed in March.

The report also said that if the Pentagon did not cover medical procedures like hormone therapy and surgery, transgender service members would probably not seek medical care and could have higher rates of substance abuse and suicide.

Making the announcement on Thursday, Mr. Carter said the Pentagon had studied the experience of allied countries that already allow transgender people to serve in their militaries, such as Britain, Australia and Israel. He also cited the experience of companies such as Boeing and Ford, which offer health insurance policies that cover the costs of gender transitions.

"That's up from zero companies in 2002," Mr. Carter said. "Among doctors, employers and insurance companies, providing medical care for transgender individuals is becoming common and normalized in both public and private sectors alike."

But as much as any practical concern played into the decision, Mr. Carter said it was also "a matter of principle."

"Americans who want to serve and can meet our standards should be afforded the opportunity to compete to do so," he said. "After all, our all-volunteer force is built upon having the most qualified Americans. And the profession of arms is based on honor and trust."

Transgender Troops Protected at Last

OPINION | BY THE NEW YORK TIMES | JUNE 30, 2016

SHORTLY AFTER the Pentagon began allowing openly gay people to serve in the military in 2011, a small group of transgender veterans quietly began to plan for the next battle. They thought it would take 15 years, perhaps more, for the military to openly accept transgender people in uniform.

It would be hard, they knew, to make the case that ending an anachronistic policy that labeled transgender people as perverts was not only morally right, but the smart thing to do. Transgender service members risked being fired for stepping forward and speaking up. But speak up they did, with enormous courage and a clear sense of what was fair for them — and right for the country they took an oath to protect.

On Thursday, less than five years after the gay ban was lifted, transgender troops won the same right. Secretary of Defense Ashton Carter said he concluded that allowing transgender people to serve would make the military a fairer employer and a stronger institution.

"We have to have access to 100 percent of America's population for our all-volunteer force to be able to recruit from among them the most highly qualified — and to retain them," Mr. Carter said in announcing the new policy.

Rules that are to go into effect this year will offer commanders and transgender troops clear guidance on matters ranging from medical treatment, access to restrooms, the use of pronouns and changes to a person's name and gender marker in military records. Critically, the new rules add gender identity as a protected category in the Pentagon's equal opportunity policy.

For transgender troops who are serving openly now, these changes lift a cloud of uncertainty that held back careers and gave them little recourse when they were subjected to discriminatory and sometimes hostile treatment.

Under the new policy, the Pentagon intends to start admitting openly transgender recruits a year from now. But to be eligible to enlist, transgender individuals will have to show that they have "been stable in their preferred gender" for at least 18 months and have completed all the transition-related medical treatment they expect to have.

This requirement sets an extraordinarily high bar. Transgender people often make decisions about medical treatment — which can include hormone replacement therapy and surgery — over the course of years. They should not be forced to affirm that they have completed a medical transition before enlisting if they are healthy and fit for the strenuous requirements of military life. Mr. Carter said that this part of the policy would be revised within two years, which will give the Defense Department an opportunity to establish more flexible guidelines.

These welcome changes come too late for some, including leading advocates of the movement for open transgender service. Roughly a year ago, Jess Shipps, a 31-year-old Air Force veteran who quit the military to transition, committed suicide after becoming despondent because she was out of work and out of money. Others, like Landon Wilson, a Navy intelligence expert, managed to rebuild their lives and careers after being kicked out of the military in a manner that was cruel and undignified.

Some senior military officials and a few members of Congress have expressed reservations about the new policy, questioning whether it was driven more by politics than by sound policy. They can put that question to rest by spending time with the transgender troops who are currently serving their country.

Trump Says Transgender People Will Not Be Allowed in the Military

BY JULIE HIRSCHFELD DAVIS AND HELENE COOPER | JULY 26, 2017

WASHINGTON — President Trump abruptly announced a ban on transgender people serving in the military on Wednesday, blindsiding his defense secretary and Republican congressional leaders with a snap decision that reversed a year-old policy reviled by social conservatives.

Mr. Trump made the declaration on Twitter, saying that American forces could not afford the "tremendous medical costs and disruption" of transgender service members. He said he had consulted generals and military experts, but Jim Mattis, the defense secretary, was given only a day's notice about the decision.

Mr. Trump elected to announce the ban in order to resolve a quietly brewing fight on Capitol Hill over whether taxpayer money should pay for gender transition and hormone therapy for transgender service members. The dispute had threatened to kill a $790 billion defense and security spending package scheduled for a vote this week.

But rather than addressing that narrow issue, Mr. Trump opted to upend the entire policy on transgender service members.

His decision was announced with such haste that the White House could not answer basic inquiries about how it would be carried out, including what would happen to openly transgender people on active duty. Of eight defense officials interviewed, none could say.

"That's something that the Department of Defense and the White House will have to work together as implementation takes place and is done so lawfully," Sarah Huckabee Sanders, the White House press secretary, said.

Still, the announcement pleased elements of Mr. Trump's base who have been dismayed to see the president break so bitterly in recent days with Attorney General Jeff Sessions, a hard-line conservative.

Civil rights and transgender advocacy groups denounced the policy, with some vowing to challenge it in court. Pentagon officials expressed dismay that the president's tweets could open them to lawsuits.

The ban would reverse the gradual transformation of the military under President Barack Obama, whose administration announced last year that transgender people could serve openly in the military. Mr. Obama's defense secretary, Ashton B. Carter, also opened all combat roles to women and appointed the first openly gay Army secretary.

And it represented a stark turnabout for Mr. Trump, who billed himself during the campaign as an ally of gay, lesbian, bisexual and transgender people.

The president, Ms. Sanders said, had concluded that allowing transgender people to serve openly "erodes military readiness and unit cohesion, and made the decision based on that."

Mr. Mattis, who was on vacation, was silent on the new policy. People close to the defense secretary said he was appalled that Mr. Trump chose to unveil his decision in tweets, in part because of the message they sent to transgender active-duty service members, including those deployed overseas, that they were suddenly no longer welcome.

The policy would affect only a small portion of the approximately 1.3 million active-duty members of the military. Some 2,000 to 11,000 active-duty troops are transgender, according to a 2016 RAND Corporation study commissioned by the Pentagon, though estimates of the number of transgender service members have varied widely, and are sometimes as high as 15,000.

The study found that allowing transgender people to serve openly in the military would "have minimal impact on readiness and health care costs" for the Pentagon. It estimated that health care costs would rise $2.4 million to $8.4 million a year, representing an infinitesimal 0.04 to 0.13 percent increase in spending. Citing research into other countries that allow transgender people to serve, the study projected "little or no impact on unit cohesion, operational effectiveness or readiness" in the United States.

Lt. Commander Blake Dremann, a Navy supply corps officer who is transgender, said he found out his job was in danger when he turned on CNN on Wednesday morning. Commander Dremann came out as transgender to his commanders in 2015, and said they had been supportive of him.

He refused to criticize Mr. Trump — "we don't criticize our commander in chief," he said — but said the policy shift "is singling out a specific population in the military, who had been assured we were doing everything appropriate to continue our honorable service."

He added: "And I will continue to do so, until the military tells me to hang up my boots."

The announcement came amid the debate on Capitol Hill over the Obama-era practice of requiring the Pentagon to pay for medical treatment related to gender transition. Representative Vicky Hartzler, Republican of Missouri, has proposed an amendment to the spending bill that would bar the Pentagon from spending money on transition surgery or related hormone therapy, and other Republicans have pressed for similar provisions.

Mr. Mattis had worked behind the scenes to keep such language out of legislation, quietly lobbying Republican lawmakers not to attach the prohibitions, according to congressional and defense officials.

But Mr. Trump was concerned that the transgender medical care issue could imperil the security spending measure, which also contains $1.6 billion for the border wall that he has championed, and wanted to resolve the dispute cleanly and straightforwardly, according to a person familiar with his thinking, who insisted on anonymity to describe it. That prompted his ban.

Republican congressional leaders were aware Mr. Trump was looking into whether taxpayer money should be spent on medical procedures for transgender service members, but had not expected him to go so far as to bar transgender people from serving altogether.

Mr. Trump and Republican lawmakers had come under pressure from Tony Perkins, the president of the Family Research Council, a leading Christian conservative group, and an ally of Mr. Trump's. Mr. Perkins opposed the bill over spending on transgender medical costs and lobbied lawmakers to do the same.

"Grant repentance to President Trump and Secretary Mattis for even considering to keep this wicked policy in place," the Family Research Council said in one of its daily prayers last week. "Grant them understanding, courage and willpower to stand up to the forces of darkness that gave birth to it and wholly to repeal it."

Opponents of allowing openly transgender service members had raised a number of concerns, including what they said was the questionable psychological fitness of those troops. They said the military was being used for social experimentation at the expense of national security.

"This was Ash Carter on his way out the door pulling the pin on a cultural grenade," Mr. Perkins said on Wednesday. "Our military leaders are saying this doesn't help make us a better fighting force; it's a distraction; it's taking up limited resources."

Mr. Carter objected to the decision, for its effect on the military and on those considering joining.

"To choose service members on other grounds than military qualifications is social policy and has no place in our military," he said in a statement. "There are already transgender individuals who are serving capably and honorably. This action would also send the wrong signal to a younger generation thinking about military service."

While some conservative lawmakers, including Ms. Hartzler, praised Mr. Trump, the president drew bipartisan condemnation on Capitol Hill and outrage from civil rights and transgender advocacy groups.

"There is no reason to force service members who are able to fight, train and deploy to leave the military — regardless of their gender identity," said Senator John McCain, Republican of Arizona and the chairman of the Senate Armed Services Committee.

He called Mr. Trump's move "yet another example of why major policy announcements should not be made via Twitter."

Senator Jack Reed, Democrat of Rhode Island and the ranking member of the Armed Services Committee, noted the irony of Mr. Trump's announcing the ban on the anniversary of President Harry Truman's order to desegregate the military. "President Trump is choosing to retreat in the march toward equality," he said.

In June, the administration delayed by six months a decision on whether to allow transgender recruits to join the military. At the time, Mr. Mattis said the delay would give military leaders a chance to review the shift's potential impact. Mr. Mattis's decision was seen as a pause to "finesse" the issue, one official said, not a prelude to anoutright ban.

The delay on recruits "was largely based on a disagreement on the science of how mental health care and hormone therapy for transgender individuals would help solve the medical issues that are associated with gender dysphoria," Gen. Paul Selva, the vice chairman of the Joint Chiefs of Staff, said during his reconfirmation hearing last week.

"I am an advocate of every qualified person who can meet the physical standards to serve in our uniformed services to be able to do so," he said.

Mr. Mattis, a retired Marine, has not been a major proponent of allowing transgender people to serve in the military, in part because medical accommodations, including hormone injections, could open the Defense Department to claims from other people not allowed to serve, like Type 1 diabetics, who also need regular injections.

But Mr. Mattis and the Pentagon's military leadership all seemed to have accepted that transgender people already serving in the military would be allowed to remain. A senior adviser to Mr. Mattis, Sally Donnelly, represented the Palm Center, an organization that advocated on behalf of the L.G.B.T. community in the military during the debate that led up to the Obama administration's decision to allow transgender people to serve, defense officials said.

Mr. Trump's abrupt decision is likely to end up in court; OutServe-SLDN, a nonprofit group that represents gay, lesbian, bisexual and transgender people in the military, immediately vowed to sue.

“We have transgender individuals who serve in elite SEAL teams, who are working in a time of war to defend our country, and now you’re going to kick them out?” Matthew F. Thorn, executive director of OutServe, said in an interview.

For Transgender Service Members, a Mix of Sadness, Anger and Fear

BY DAVE PHILIPPS | JULY 26, 2017

COLORADO SPRINGS — Joining the Navy was one of the best decisions Alec Kerry said she had ever made. The other was coming out as transgender.

"The Navy taught me how people can come together and work hard to achieve something bigger than themselves," said Petty Officer Kerry, 24, who is training to operate nuclear reactors and soon plans to adopt the name Eva. "Strangely enough, I think what the Navy taught us about integrity was what gave me the courage to come out. I had to be honest about who I was with myself and the people I served with."

Like thousands of other transgender veterans and members of the military, she grappled with a mix of anger, sadness and fear on Wednesday after President Trump tweeted that the United States military would no longer "accept or allow" transgender people to serve — a surprise move that came a year after the Obama administration permitted transgender troops to serve openly.

Some transgender troops were left to wonder if they would face a quick discharge from the military or if scheduled medical appointments would be canceled. And nearly all expressed dismay at what they saw as a misguided action that could purge the military of untold numbers of highly skilled and dedicated service members, bringing back an era when many troops lived in secrecy and shame.

Petty Officer Kerry, who has been taking estrogen for months, said starting to become a woman lifted a cloud that allowed her to perform better at work, but now she is likely to have to stop treatment.

"People are fearful," said Laila Ireland, who was an Army combat medic for 13 years before transitioning to a woman and becoming the membership director for Sparta, an L.G.B.T. military group with more than 500 active-duty members. "All morning I've been telling them, Continue to exceed the expectations, show what you are worth."

Her husband, Logan Ireland, an Air Force staff sergeant who is also transgender, could not be reached because he was in a combat leadership course, but said in a text message from the field, "I would love for my president to meet me," adding that he would like to tell Mr. Trump about all the "honorably serving transgender military members that are fighting right now for their liberties and for their country."

There are an estimated 2,000 to 11,000 active-duty transgender service members, according to a 2016 RAND Corporation study commissioned by the Pentagon. Since the Obama administration lifted the ban on transgender people serving, public opinion has been mixed. A poll conducted by Rasmussen Reports in June found that 23 percent of those surveyed believed that having them serve openly was good for the military, 38 percent said it would have no impact and 31 percent said it would hurt.

But enlisting transgender people and paying for their medical transition has become a political flash point, and there has been strong resistance. A monument to transgender veterans unveiled in June at Abraham Lincoln National Cemetery in Illinois was almost immediately defaced by vandals.

"I thought we were at a place of progress, and it feels like we're taking 10 steps back," said Umut Dursun, 35, a former Marine in Miami who transitioned from female to male after his service. He was sitting in a V.A. waiting room on Wednesday morning when he saw the news. "We're not afraid of bullets flying at us," he said. "But we are afraid of someone's experience around gender because we don't understand it."

Some conservatives say transgender troops require too many medical procedures that would undermine the military's fighting capability, and they hailed Wednesday's announcement.

Tony Perkins, a Marine veteran who is now president of the Family Research Council, a conservative advocacy group, issued a statement praising Mr. Trump "for keeping his promise to return to military priorities — and not continue the social experimentation of the Obama era that has crippled our nation's military."

Representative Vicky Hartzler, Republican of Missouri, recently offered an amendment that would have barred the military from paying for sex reassignment surgery. In a statement, Ms. Hartzler praised Mr. Trump for taking "decisive action."

"With the challenges we are facing across the globe, we are asking the American people to invest their hard-earned money in national defense," she said. "Each dollar needs to be spent to address threats facing our nation."

Transgender troops pushed back hard on the medical cost arguments, noting that the estimated $2.4 million to $8.4 million a year it would cost for care was a fraction of the $41 million the Department of Defense spent on Viagra in 2014.

One National Guard intelligence sergeant named Mac, who did not want to give his full name because he now fears being discharged, worried that the cost of investigations to ferret out closeted transgender troops could eclipse the costs of providing medical care, and in the process drive away career service members.

"The government has invested hundreds of thousand of dollars into my training and my skill set," he said. "That's not easy to replace."

Traditional veterans groups, including the Veterans of Foreign Wars and the American Legion, whose memberships tend to be older and more conservative, have been silent on the issue, but Iraq and Afghanistan Veterans of America, which represents the newest generation of fighters, came out strongly against the president's position.

"This is backward, harmful and contrary to American values. It's also bad for national security," said Paul Rieckhoff, the group's founder. "Thousands of transgender troops are serving in our military right now. An unknown number are in combat zones today."

Some young troops said they often did not know they were transgender before they joined, and developed a sense of service and of self that now feel inseparably bound.

"At lot of us grew up not really feeling we belonged," said Staff Sgt. Ashlee Bruce of the Air Force, who dresses as female at home but at work uses her birth name, Matthew. "The military took us and made us part of a team. They said, Hey, you are important to us."

Like many others interviewed, Sergeant Bruce said commanders and peers had shown nothing but support when she announced, after a deployment to Africa, that she was transitioning. Buckley Air Force Base in Colorado, where the sergeant works, even had her do a public service video about her experience.

Sergeant Bruce is scheduled to be evaluated for hormone therapy in a few weeks. If, instead, she is discharged, she said she would have no regrets because the military helped her realize who she wants to be.

"I love the Air Force," she said. "And I owe the Air Force a debt. I'm going to keep coming into work every day and doing the best I can until they tell me don't come to work any more."

JULIE TURKEWITZ CONTRIBUTED REPORTING FROM DENVER, SHERYL GAY STOLBERG FROM WASHINGTON, AND KIRK JOHNSON FROM SEATTLE. SUSAN C. BEACHY CONTRIBUTED RESEARCH.

Trump's Contempt for Transgender Heroes

OPINION | BY JENNIFER FINNEY BOYLAN | JULY 26, 2017

LAST YEAR, there was a reunion of the crew of the U.S.S. Francis Scott Key. The submarine had been launched in 1966, and was part of the Navy's nuclear fleet until its decommissioning in 1993.

Machinist Mate First Class Monica Helms was nervous about going to the reunion. She'd served on the Francis Scott Key as well as on another sub for eight years. But she'd come out as transgender since that time. It wasn't clear how her shipmates would react.

She needn't have worried. "It was an amazing experience," she told me. "We were just shipmates, that's all it was." Thirty years later, there was still a sense of loyalty, not only to the country, but to the people with whom she had served.

"The fact that we were all doing the same work, experiencing the same stress, going through the same problems, that put you on the same level as them. They see that you are willing to do the job, and you can do it, and they are fine with that. They trust you."

I spoke with Ms. Helms on Wednesday, about an hour after President Trump announced, in a series of tweets, that transgender people are not welcome in America's military, reversing a movement toward open and unashamed service initiated during the Obama administration.

No, thank you, President Trump. Thank you for making it clear, once again, that you were lying during the campaign when you tweeted to L.G.B.T. people: "I will fight for you while Hillary brings in more people that will threaten your freedoms and beliefs."

Transgender Americans have served and are serving courageously in our military. "I came from a long line of people who have served in this country," said Ms. Helms. "To have someone say to me, I'm not worthy to be allowed to serve, simply because I'm different, is a horrible and bigoted way of looking at things."

The statement isn't just horrible and bigoted. It's also inaccurate. Trans medical costs to the military are not "tremendous" — they are negligible.

A RAND study commissioned by the former defense secretary Ashton B. Carter found that transgender service members would "cost little and have no significant impact on unit readiness." It estimated that paying for active-duty members to transition would cost $2.9 million to $4.2 million a year. The study also found that there are around 2,450 transgender active-duty service members (though other estimates go above 15,000). What will these people do now?

And as for "disruption" — that's how some people in the last century viewed the military service of African-Americans.

In fact, "today is the anniversary of President Truman fully integrating black Americans into the military," Amanda Simpson, a former deputy assistant secretary of defense who also happens to be transgender, pointed out to me. "It's abhorrent and disrespectful that President Trump would choose this anniversary to discriminate against our service members," she continued. "He's picked on the most vulnerable people to create a distraction, but he's picked on the wrong people — he's picked on service members."

The country's armed forces reflect not only the kind of country that we are, but the one we wish to become. In speaking of the service of black American in World War II, Bill De Shields, a retired Army colonel, once said, "The symbol of black participation at that time was 'the Double V.' " That meant "victory against the enemy abroad, and victory against the enemy at home. The enemy at home of course being racism, discrimination, prejudice and Jim Crow."

For trans people, the enemy at home is alive and well; just last week the Texas Legislature convened a special session in order to try to enshrine anti-trans bigotry into law. Discrimination is a threat not just to trans Americans but to all of us who live in a country in which one group of people is told that they do not belong.

As a co-chair of Glaad, I spent Wednesday morning hearing from dozens of vets struggling with the sense that the country they served does not value their lives.

Vandy Beth Glenn, a former Naval officer, said she joined the Navy "to serve and protect the nation and the system of government that stood for so many ideals I cherished: freedom, equality, a guarantee of various rights." She continued, "I don't believe Donald Trump feels anything but contempt for transgender Americans — or any human beings beyond his immediate family."

More and more transgender service members have begun coming out before retiring. Jessie Armentrout, a Naval engineer, said that "being transgender did not affect my ability to serve my country with honor." She went on, "I served this country to protect everyone's rights and freedoms and one would think that would include my own."

For what possible reason, in 2017, should we turn back progress toward equality? If the president is truly focused on "decisive and overwhelming victory," should that fight not include victory over the forces of bigotry and ignorance?

After her service on the Francis Scott Key, Monica Helms went on to create the transgender flag — a set of pink, blue and white stripes. "The pattern is such that no matter which way you fly it, it is always correct, signifying us finding correctness in our lives."

A few years ago, the flag was acquired by the Smithsonian Institution, turning Machinist Mate First Class Helms into a kind of transgender Betsy Ross. On the occasion of that acquisition, Ms. Helms said with pride, "It tells the world that trans people are part of this country."

The message that the president sent out today tells the world the opposite.

Chelsea Manning: President Trump, Trans People in the Military Are Here to Stay

OPINION | BY CHELSEA MANNING | JULY 27, 2017

WITH THREE TWEETS, the leader of the largest employer in the country just tried to lay off all trans people in the military. Many service members who were just told "we want you" are suddenly being told "go away." The sudden reversal by the administration, from allowing trans people to serve openly in the military to outright banning us, is a devastating blow to our livelihoods, our basic humanity, our survival. It is also a devastating blow to the entire credibility of the United States military for years to come.

This is all painfully familiar. Once upon a time, I was denied the ability to even exist as who I am. I had to hide. I had to be in the closet. I had to lie to people I stood next to. I had to virtually eradicate my own existence from myself. I served as a gay person under "don't ask, don't tell," and also as a trans person under the ban on open transgender service. I came out as trans only during my years working as an analyst in the Army.

So, here we are again. After years of advocacy, research, experts' weighing-in, lives lost, we made progress. And now, again, we are hurtling backward. We are risking our credibility, our legitimacy as a nation and, again, risking the lives of so many people who are listening and watching, and who are already serving.

There is a lot of hurt. There is a lot of fear. Trans people even outside the military are terrified about what this means for the rest of us. Terrible discriminatory laws targeting trans people are proposed all across the country, and now the commander in chief of the armed forces is propagating lies about us, dehumanizing us and taking away our health care and employment.

What does this mean? Well, for now we don't exactly know, since it is clear that the president's tweets were not exactly well thought out. But it could mean that trans people will have to pack up and go home for pretty much no reason other than "you can't stay here." For no other reason than, we feel like using you as political pawns today, or we don't understand you, or you simply are not welcome here.

Money is the excuse today. It was supposed to be expensive to provide trans people with adequate health care. The reality is that the costs are negligible. Military spending wastes billions of dollars on projects that are canceled or don't work, every day.

Medicine was the old excuse. The old military regulations were laced with medical terms to justify discrimination. They psychopathologized us trans people as having "manifestations" of "paraphilias," and "psychosexual conditions, transsexual, gender identity disorder to include major abnormalities or defects of the genitalia such as change of sex or a current attempt to change sex," that would "render an individual administratively unfit" to serve.

These old regulations could come back. The rhetoric about trans people having "mental disorders" could come back, too. It's the same thing we see in state houses across the country. Trans people are "mentally ill." We are "predators." We are the ethereal enemy of the moment. Even though there is a medical consensus, a legal consensus, a military consensus that none of this is true.

This is about bias and prejudice. This is about systemic discrimination. Like the integration of people of color and women in the past, this was a sign of progress that threatens the social order, and the president is reacting against that progress.

But we will move forward. We will make sure that all trans people in the military, and all people outside the military after serving, receive the medical care they need. We will not back down. Our progress will continue. Our organizing and activism will grow stronger.

We are neither disruptive nor expensive. We are human beings, and we will not be erased or ignored.

I Am a Transgender Female Captain in the U.S. Army

OPINION | BY JENNIFER SIMS | JULY 27, 2017

HOHENFELS, GERMANY — My eyes welled with tears of happiness, and I cried as I had never cried before. For 20 years, I fought against who I am. But that day was the closest I ever felt to freedom. It was June 30, 2016, and Secretary of Defense Ashton Carter had just announced an end to the United States military's ban on transgender service.

My name is Jennifer Sims. I am a United States Army captain and a transgender woman who has served my country with distinction for more than six years. I am speaking for myself here, not on behalf of the Army or the government, but I suspect my feelings resonate with other transgender service members.

Every transgender person has a different story. For me, growing up in Florida and Minnesota, I never felt right as a boy, struggling to conform to what that meant. It was before the internet and smartphones were everywhere, so I never heard the word "transgender" or had any way to look up confidentially what I was feeling. I thought it was simply a phase I was going through.

Like many transgender women before they come out, I tried to act as masculine as I could. I played every sport possible, and always tried to be the strongest, fastest boy on the playground. My family has a history of military service, so I told people my dream was to be in the Army. What could be manlier than joining the military? In my sophomore year at Florida Atlantic University, I joined Army R.O.T.C. I also finally began to accept myself, but I didn't come to the conclusion that I am transgender until 2010, almost a year after I had committed to an Army R.O.T.C. scholarship.

My choices were simple, yet complex: serve the nation or serve myself. On the one hand, I no longer felt the need to act supermasculine in my life, and I saw a path forward. On the other, I saw a nation at war and I wanted to help. In the end, I couldn't resist the call to serve. In 2011, I graduated and accepted my commission as a second lieutenant in the Army. Eight months later, I was in Afghanistan managing communications for an aviation task force in Zabul Province.

For more than four years, I suppressed my secret. Living a lie left me utterly exhausted, but the worst part was never being able to talk to anyone about what I was feeling. I had served in Afghanistan, Indonesia and Germany, and my mental health was deteriorating. I was depressed and found little enjoyment in life.

That all changed in July 2015 when the Department of Defense announced that it would begin studying open transgender service. I came out to my family, and when I could, I started living more of my life as myself. It wasn't perfect, though, as I had to continue keeping this hidden at work. A military unit is like a living being, and a senior leader coming out as transgender in the wrong way could become a self-destructive virus. I felt it was my duty to keep anything about being transgender from making its way into the workplace until the time was right.

The day the policy officially changed I immediately sought medical care but had to wait while everyone in the Army became familiar with the new guidelines. In November 2016, I began my medical transition. Each day was better than the one before, but it wasn't until last April that I felt true freedom for the first time. In consultation with my commander, I came out to my unit. Although some were slow to accept me, there have not been any disruptions to the unit's operations because of my revelation.

I'm pleased that the chairman of the Joint Chiefs of Staff is seeking to clarify President Trump's announcement on Wednesday about barring transgender people from serving in the military. But I won't feed the expected narrative about the commander in chief ending my dreams of a military career; I'm ready for civilian life when my commitment is up and focused on attending law school. I will simply say that, from what I have experienced, open transgender service strengthens our military. Enabling soldiers to pursue their gender identity allows them to feel a part of the Army's team and empowers them to be all they can be. Every soldier deserves to have that experience, including the thousands who are transgender.

The last two years, the years I've been transitioning, have been the most productive so far of my eight-year commitment to the Army, and I can only imagine what else I could have accomplished if I had felt unencumbered during those first four years. Despite everything I've been through, and regardless of my future plans, until the day I am no longer in uniform, I will continue contributing everything I can in service of the nation.

Trump Cites Familiar Argument in Ban on Transgender Troops

BY HELENE COOPER | AUG. 3, 2017

WASHINGTON — When President Trump chose Twitter last week to announce that he planned to ban transgender service members from the military, he said his decision would safeguard the readiness of the armed forces and was made on the advice of his generals.

Now, a week after Mr. Trump's Twitter statements, military policy experts say that years of study have not produced much evidence to support Mr. Trump's claims that transgender service members make it harder for the American military to focus on "decisive and overwhelming victory," as the president wrote.

A group of 56 retired generals and admirals put out a statement this week saying that ejecting transgender service members would itself degrade military readiness. In true Washington form, the 56 were answering a letter from another group of 16 retired generals that said Mr. Trump's proposed ban was necessary "to save the culture and war-fighting capacity of the U.S. military."

The White House has still not put forward a serving general or military adviser to publicly back Mr. Trump's assertion. Defense Secretary Jim Mattis has been quiet on the topic, and Gen. Joseph F. Dunford Jr., the chairman of the Joint Chiefs of Staff, said the military was not kicking out any service members until the White House sent specific guidelines. The commandant of the Coast Guard, Adm. Paul F. Zukunft, said on Tuesday that he would continue to support transgender troops under his command.

The military readiness argument is a familiar one.

It was used in 1948 when the issue was opening up the military ranks to blacks (impairing "the morale of the Army at a time when our armed forces should be at their strongest and most efficient," warned Senator J. Lister Hill, Democrat of Alabama); in the 1990s, when the issue was allowing women into combat ("females have biological problems staying in a ditch for 30 days because they get infections," said Representative Newt Gingrich, Republican of Georgia); and in 2010, when the issue was allowing gays to serve openly in the military (it would "harm the battle effectiveness which is so vital to the survival of our young men and women in the military," asserted Senator John McCain, Republican of Arizona).

Now, Mr. Trump is making another grab at the readiness defense. The American military, he said on Twitter, "cannot be burdened with the tremendous medical costs and disruption that transgender in the military would entail."

Critics of allowing transgender service members in the military say they will indeed add to overall medical costs and increase the number of active duty personnel who are out of commission for medical reasons. They point to Army statistics indicating that, at any one time, around 50,000 of the service's approximately 500,000 personnel are on some manner of sick leave, with reasons ranging from a bad knee to maternity leave. That 10 percent nondeployable rate, commanders say, affects readiness.

Because many transgender people undergo hormone therapy or surgery to transition to the gender with which they identify, these service members often need more medical care than other military recruits.

Brad Carson, who was acting undersecretary of defense for personnel and readiness in 2015 and 2016, when the issue of allowing transgender members was being debated, said officials representing the Army and the Marines expressed worries about adding to what they saw as an already high number of people on medical leave.

"They would say, so now you're telling me we're going to admit a cohort of people who almost by definition will need medical care," Mr. Carson said, recalling the extensive meetings at the Pentagon on how opening the military to transgender people would affect readiness. "They already thought they didn't have enough people to man the units. Their view was, we need to get that number down from 50,000, so they would support nothing that added to it, including maternity leave expansion."

Those arguments were rejected in a report by the RAND Corporation, released in May 2016, which found that allowing transgender people to serve would "cost little and have no significant impact on unit readiness."

The study estimated that 2,450 active-duty members were transgender, predicted that around 65 would seek to transition each year, and estimated that the cost to the Pentagon would be $2.9 million to $4.2 million a year.

"So the Army had 50,000 people out of commission," Mr. Carson said, recalling the arguments that allowing transgender troops to serve would not affect readiness. "The number of people we would be adding would be minuscule. People are in and out of readiness status anyway. We have long experience in giving people hormone

JUSTIN GILLILAND/THE NEW YORK TIMES

Protesters outside the White House after President Trump announced on Twitter that transgender troops would not be allowed to serve in the military.

treatments — men can get low testosterone treatments; women can get birth control pills."

And the medical costs would also be small in the context of a $600 billion annual budget.

The argument that allowing a new cohort of recruits would harm military readiness was ultimately rejected in the case of allowing African-Americans in the 1940s, women in combat in the 1990s and gays and lesbians in 2010.

In most of such cases, the military arrived at desegregation before other parts of the government and American society as a whole.

"Because the military pulls from all parts of the country, it's forced to deal with the same issues as the rest of society," said Eric Fanning, the first openly gay man to serve as Army secretary. "Oftentimes, it's made to confront these issues earlier and more directly than society at large. And as a result, the military often helps lead the way for change."

5 Transgender Service Members Sue Trump Over Military Ban

BY CHARLIE SAVAGE | AUG. 9, 2017

WASHINGTON — Five transgender people serving in the United States military sued President Trump and top Pentagon officials on Wednesday, asking that transgender troops be allowed to stay in the military.

The lawsuit was filed in response to Mr. Trump's ban abruptly announced last month on Twitter.

The plaintiffs filed the lawsuit under pseudonyms — "Jane Doe" Nos. 1-5 — in the United States District Court for the District of Columbia. The case was organized by two rights groups, the National Center for Lesbian Rights and GLBTQ Legal Advocates & Defenders, or GLAD.

Other rights groups — like Lambda, Outserve and the American Civil Liberties Union — have also said they are preparing lawsuits but are holding off until the Trump administration takes a step to put the ban into effect, such as issuing formal guidance to the military or beginning the process of changing military rules.

But Shannon Minter, the legal director for the National Center for Lesbian Rights, said he believed the case was already ripe for a lawsuit because active transgender service members — such as those deciding whether to re-enlist — were already being harmed by the uncertainty created by Mr. Trump's statements on Twitter.

"It is critical to act now because the harms are happening now," Mr. Minter said. "These service members deserve to know where they stand."

A 2014 study by the Williams Institute at the University of California, Los Angeles, estimated that about 8,800 transgender people were serving on active duty, with thousands more in the National Guard and reserve; a 2016 study by the RAND Corporation estimated that there were about 2,450 such active-duty troops. In 2016, the Obama administration, after extensive study, lifted a prior ban on transgender troops. That permitted transgender members currently serving to come out openly; openly transgender people are set to be allowed to join the military starting next year.

But on July 26, without warning, Mr. Trump stated on Twitter that the government "will not accept or allow transgender individuals to serve in any capacity in the U.S. Military." The announcement caught the military off guard, and there was no plan for what to do about those now serving openly.

Gen. Joseph F. Dunford Jr., the chairman of the Joint Chiefs of Staff, responded to Mr. Trump's Twitter statements by saying the current policy about who was allowed to serve had not changed and would remain in place until the White House sent the Defense Department new rules and Jim Mattis, the defense secretary, issued new guidelines.

"In the meantime, we will continue to treat all of our personnel with respect," General Dunford said in a letter to the military service chiefs.

On Aug. 4, The Blade, a newspaper for lesbian, gay, bisexual and transgender people, reported, citing unnamed sources, that a policy guidance for reinstating the ban had been approved by the White House counsel's office and by Mr. Trump and was expected to be delivered to Mr. Mattis.

Mr. Minter said that based on that report, "We wanted to move as quickly as possible to nip that in the bud." The lawsuit's complaint stated that "upon information and belief, the White House turned that decision into official guidance, approved by the White House counsel's office, to be communicated to the Department of Defense."

Still, as of Wednesday, the White House had yet to send any specific policy directive to the Pentagon, said Lt. Col. Paul Haverstick, a military spokesman. He said General Dunford's statement from two weeks ago remained in effect.

"There is no change," he said. "We are still waiting for more guidance from the White House."

The lawsuit complaint argued that banning transgender people from serving in the military would be unconstitutional discrimination, violating their rights to equal protection and due process. It also argued that the Pentagon could not end people's military careers for coming out openly as transgender because they did so in relying on the Pentagon itself saying they would be permitted to serve.

Colonel Haverstick said the military was "aware of the lawsuit; however, we are not able to comment due to the pending litigation."

Other rights groups preparing similar legal challenges said on Wednesday that they were still holding off. Among them are both Outserve and Lambda, which have said they are recruiting plaintiffs for a joint lawsuit when the matter is ripe, a legal term meaning the facts of a case have developed enough for a decision.

"We have not yet filed suit, although we stand ready to do so," Jon Davidson, the Lambda legal director, said on Wednesday. "We have been awaiting confirmation that the White House has transmitted a final guidance, directive or other instructions to the Department of Defense, which, to the best of our knowledge, has not yet occurred."

James D. Esseks, director of the American Civil Liberties Union's Lesbian Gay Bisexual Transgender & HIV Project, said that his group was also holding back, but noted that it had sent a letter to the White House asking it to preserve all documents related to the matter in anticipation of future litigation.

Even if the administration has not yet transformed Mr. Trump's Twitter announcement into policy, it remains possible that it will do so by the time a judge has to decide whether the new lawsuit is ripe for adjudication or should be dismissed, experts said.

Regardless, Mr. Minter expressed confidence that the suit had not been filed too quickly. He noted that defending against the case would force the White House to talk about the status of plans to reinstate the ban, and he argued that there was "no downside" to a strategy of moving ahead now.

"I don't think we will get dismissed on ripeness because people are being harmed now," he said. "But if we do, we will be right back as soon as there is any additional movement."

Judge Blocks Trump's Ban on Transgender Troops in Military

BY DAVE PHILIPPS | OCT. 30, 2017

A FEDERAL JUDGE on Monday temporarily blocked a White House policy barring military service by transgender troops, ruling that it was based on "disapproval of transgender people generally."

Judge Colleen Kollar-Kotelly of the Federal District Court for the District of Columbia found the administration's justification for the ban, which was set to take effect in March 2018, to be suspect and likely unconstitutional. She ruled that the military's current policy should remain in place.

"There is absolutely no support for the claim that the ongoing service of transgender people would have any negative effective on the military at all," the judge wrote in a strongly worded, 76-page ruling. "In fact, there is considerable evidence that it is the discharge and banning of such individuals that would have such effects."

Judge Kollar-Kotelly noted that the White House's proposed policies likely violated the equal protection clause of the Constitution, writing that "a number of factors — including the sheer breadth of the exclusion ordered by the directives, the unusual circumstances surrounding the President's announcement of them, the fact that the reasons given for them do not appear to be supported by any facts, and the recent rejection of those reasons by the military itself — strongly suggest that Plaintiffs' Fifth Amendment claim is meritorious."

Monday's ruling was seen as an encouraging step for supporters. It stops a plan to discharge all transgender troops, allows current transgender troops to re-enlist and permits transgender recruits to join the military starting in January.

"She basically wiped the slate clean," said Shannon Minter, a lawyer at the National Center for Lesbian Rights who represented the plaintiffs, adding that while the ruling could be appealed, he was confident that it effectively marked the end of the ban because the judge said it violated the Constitution.

Judge Kollar-Kotelly did not impose an injunction on the ban on sex reassignment surgery because she said it did not apply to any of the plaintiffs. But the plaintiffs' lawyers argued that in blocking the entire policy, the ruling effectively shelved the ban on sex reassignment surgery as well.

In a statement, the Justice Department said, "We disagree with the court's ruling and are currently evaluating the next steps."

President Trump announced in a series of Twitter messages in July that American forces could not afford the "tremendous medical costs and disruption" of transgender troops, and said "the United States Government will not accept or allow them to serve in any capacity in the U.S. Military." A presidential memorandum released in August required all transgender service members to be discharged starting in March 2018.

The announcement blindsided many in the military, which had been moving ahead with plans to integrate transgender troops, based on a 2016 study commissioned by the military that found that allowing transgender people to serve openly would "have minimal impact on readiness and health care costs" for the Pentagon.

It estimated that health care costs would rise $2.4 million to $8.4 million a year, representing an almost unnoticeable 0.04 to 0.13 percent increase in spending. The study also projected "little or no impact on unit cohesion, operational effectiveness or readiness."

Civil rights groups immediately sued the administration on behalf of transgender service members, arguing that the ban was discriminatory and violated their constitutional right to due process and equal protection under the law. A number of lawsuits are still pending.

The government had asked that the case be dismissed, but Judge Kollar-Kotelly denied the motion, writing that while "perhaps compelling in the abstract," the government's arguments for dismissal "wither away under scrutiny." Judge Kollar-Kotelly was nominated to a lower court in the District of Columbia by President Ronald Reagan and was named to the federal bench by President Bill Clinton.

The suit was filed by GLBTQ Legal Advocates and Defenders and the National Center for Lesbian Rights on behalf of five unnamed transgender women serving in the Coast Guard, Army and Air Force. Many of the women had served for years as men and had been deployed to war zones before coming out to commanders when the ban was lifted in 2016. One is a few years from retirement, according to court documents. Another told her commander she wanted to keep serving, but would resign if the military moved to forcibly discharge her.

"Big, huge news today," said Lt. Cmdr. Blake Dremann, a Navy supply corps officer who is transgender and is the director of Sparta, an L.G.B.T. military group with more than 650 active-duty members. "A lot of people's lives were put on hold. They thought their careers were ending. This means we can continue to serve with honor, as we have been doing."

Petty Officer Eva Kerry, 24, who is transgender and is training to operate nuclear reactors, said the ruling lifted an obsessive dread over the impending end of a Navy career she loves. "I remain optimistic that the Constitution I swore an oath to will continue to protect the rights of all Americans," she said on Monday.

The decision is the latest in a series of controversial White House policies halted by the courts, including limiting travel from predominantly Muslim countries and withholding federal grant money from so-called sanctuary cities. Asked for comment, Sarah Huckabee Sanders, the White House press secretary, said the Justice Department was reviewing the ruling.

The lawsuit is premature, the Justice Department said, because "none of the plaintiffs have established that they will be impacted by current policies on military service."

The decision is a blow for social conservatives, who have pushed to curtail transgender policies since the ban was lifted in 2016. In June, some Republicans in Congress unsuccessfully sought to force a ban

AL DRAGO/THE NEW YORK TIMES

People gathered outside the White House during a protest for transgender rights on Wednesday.

on sex reassignment surgery by attaching it to the annual military spending bill. In response, Mr. Trump made a far bolder move to ban transgender service members entirely.

At the time, Representative Vicky Hartzler, a Republican from Missouri, openly praised what she said was the president's willingness to put national security first. On Monday, her press secretary said she would not comment on the ruling.

Democrats in Congress, who in September introduced legislation to protect transgender troops from discharge, were quick to mark a victory.

"Federal courts have again beat back the sinister specter of discrimination bred within the Trump White House," Senator Richard Blumenthal of Connecticut said in a statement. "This court order will allow our transgender troops to continue serving based on their ability to fight, train, and deploy — regardless of gender identity."

Logan Ireland, an Air Force staff sergeant who was not involved in the lawsuits, said he and other transgender troops were hopeful but cautious. He said the president could still take steps to discharge them.

More than anything, the Afghanistan veteran, who leads security forces, said he hoped the end of the ban would allow him to concentrate more on his work.

"We want to go back to serving," he said. "There are troops that work under me, there is work to be done. We want to do it. After all, we are here for our country, not who sits in the White House."

Glossary

advocate One who upholds or defends the cause or interests of a group.

bathroom bill (or law) The common name for a piece of legislation that regulates access to public facilities — specifically restrooms — for transgender individuals.

bigotry Intolerance toward those who hold different opinions from oneself.

cisgender A person whose gender matches the sex they were assigned at birth.

discriminatory Prejudicial or unfair toward an individual or group of individuals on the basis of unchangeable qualities, such as gender or race.

"don't ask, don't tell" The policy that banned openly gay and lesbian troops from serving in the military from 1993-2011.

gay Men expressing a sexual or romantic preference for other men, or more generally attraction to people of the same sex or gender.

gender dysphoria A medical term to describe the distress or depression produced by a gap between one's gender identity and their assigned birth gender.

gender identity A person's perception of one's own gender. It may or may not correlate with the assigned sex at birth.

gentrification The process of urban renewal and renovation of deteriorating neighborhoods, often involving the displacement of lower-class residents and an influx of middle- or upper-class residents.

innate Inherent; belonging to the nature of something.

lesbian A woman who expresses a sexual or romantic preference for other women.

misgender To refer to someone using a pronoun that does not correspond to their gender identity.

ordinance A law or regulation set forth by a municipal authority.

right Something that one may justly claim as theirs.

Title IX The federal civil rights law that prevents discrimination based on sex or gender in public schools.

transgender Describes an individual whose gender identity is inconsistent with the gender they were assigned at birth.

transgender man A person who identifies as a man but was assigned female at birth.

transgender woman A person who identifies as a woman but was assigned male at birth.

transition To adopt permanently the outward or physical characteristics of the gender one identifies with, as opposed to those associated with one's birth sex.

transphobia Irrational discrimination against or hatred or fear of transgender individuals.

Media Literacy Terms

"Media literacy" refers to the ability to access, understand, critically assess, and create media. The following terms are important components of media literacy, and they will help you critically engage with the articles in this title.

angle The aspect of a news story that a journalist focuses on and develops.

attribution The method by which a source is identified or by which facts and information are assigned to the person who provided them.

balance The principle of journalism that both perspectives of an argument should be presented in a fair way.

bias A disposition of prejudice in favor of a certain idea, person or perspective.

byline The name of the writer, usually placed between the headline and the story.

chronological order A method of writing a story presenting the details of the story in the order in which they occurred.

column A type of story that is a regular feature, often on a recurring topic, written by the same journalist, generally known as a columnist.

commentary A type of story that is an expression of opinion on recent events by a journalist generally known as a commentator.

credibility The quality of being trustworthy and believable, said of a journalistic source.

editorial An article of opinion or interpretation.

feature story An article designed to entertain as well as to inform.

headline Type, usually 18 point or larger, used to introduce a story.

human interest story A type of story that focuses on individuals and how events or issues affect their life, generally offering a sense of relatability to the reader.

impartiality The principle of journalism that a story should not reflect a journalist's bias and should contain balance.

intention The motive or reason behind something, such as the publication of a news story.

motive The reason behind something, such as the publication of a news story or a source's perspective on an issue.

news story An article or style of expository writing that reports news, generally in a straightforward fashion and without editorial comment.

op-ed An opinion piece that reflects a prominent journalist's opinion on a topic of interest.

paraphrase The summary of an individual's words, with attribution, rather than a direct quotation of their exact words.

plagiarism An attempt to pass another person's work off as one's own without attribution.

quotation The use of an individual's exact words indicated by the use of quotation marks and proper attribution.

reliability The quality of being dependable and accurate, said of a journalistic source.

source The origin of the information reported in journalism.

tone A manner of expression in writing or speech.

Media Literacy Questions

1. Identify the various sources cited in the article "N.B.A. to Move All-Star Game from North Carolina" (on page 155). How does the journalist attribute information to each of these sources in their article? How effective are their attributions in helping the reader identify their sources?

2. In "As Transgender Students Make Gains, Schools Hesitate at Bathrooms" (on page 78), Julie Bosman and Motoko Rich paraphrase information from David Vannasdall before quoting him. What are the strengths of the use of a paraphrase as opposed to a direct quote? What are its weaknesses?

3. Compare the headlines of "North Carolina Bans Local Anti-Discrimination Policies" (on page 146) and "Texas Bathroom Bill Has Emotions, and Stakes, Running High" (on page 159). Which is a more compelling headline, and why? How could the less compelling headline be changed to draw better the reader's interest?

4. What type of story is "Who Gets to Play the Transgender Part?" (on page 55)? Can you identify another article in this collection that is the same type of story?

5. Does Adam Liptak demonstrate the journalistic principle of impartiality in his article "Supreme Court Won't Hear Major Case on Transgender Rights" (on page 138)? If so, how did his do so? If not, what could he have included to make their article more impartial?

6. The article "Trump's Contempt for Transgender Heroes" (on page 190) is an example of an op-ed. Identify how Jennifer Finney Boylan's attitude, tone, and bias help convey her opinion on the topic.

7. Does "Trump Says Transgender People Will Not Be Allowed in the Military" (on page 180) use multiple sources? What are the strengths of using multiple sources in a journalistic piece? What are the weaknesses of relying heavily on one source/few sources?

8. What is the intention of the article "South Dakota Bill on Transgender Students' Bathroom Access Draws Ire" (on page 87)? How effectively does it achieve its intended purpose?

9. Analyze the authors' bias in "Activists Say Police Abuse of Transgender People Persists Despite Reforms" (on page 67) and "Beyond Caitlyn Jenner Lies a Long Struggle by Transgender People" (on page 60). Do you think one journalist is more biased in their reporting than the other? If so, why do you think so?

10. Often, as a news story develops, journalists' attitude toward the subject may change. Compare "Transgender Bathroom Debate Turns Personal at a Vermont High School" (on page 103) and "A Transgender Student Won Her Battle. Now It's War." (on page 120), both by Anemona Hartocollis. Did new information discovered between the publication of these two articles change Hartocollis's perspective?

Citations

All citations in this list are formatted according to the Modern Language Association's (MLA) style guide.

Book Citation

NEW YORK TIMES EDITORIAL STAFF, THE. *Transgender Rights: Striving for Equality.* New York Times Educational Publishing, 2019.

Article Citations

ANDREWS, MALIKA. "How Should High Schools Define Sexes for Transgender Athletes?" *The New York Times*, 8 Nov. 2017, www.nytimes.com/2017/11/08/sports/transgender-athletes.html.

ASTOR, MAGGIE. "Violence Against Transgender People Is on the Rise, Advocates Say." *The New York Times*, 9 Nov. 2017, www.nytimes.com/2017/11/09/us/transgender-women-killed.html.

BAIRD, JULIA. "The Courage of Transgender Soldiers." *The New York Times*, 21 Feb. 2014, www.nytimes.com/2014/02/22/opinion/sunday/baird-the-courage-of-trans-soldiers.html.

BARNES, BROOKS. "Who Gets to Play the Transgender Part?" *The New York Times*, 3 Sept. 2015, www.nytimes.com/2015/09/04/movies/who-gets-to-play-the-transgender-part-in-hollywood.html.

BELLAFANTE, GINA. "Poor, Transgender and Dressed for Arrest." *The New York Times*, 30 Sept. 2016, www.nytimes.com/2016/10/02/nyregion/poor-transgender-and-dressed-for-arrest.html.

BENNETT, JESSICA. "She? Ze? They? What's in a Gender Pronoun." *The New York Times*, 30 Jan. 2016, www.nytimes.com/2016/01/31/fashion/pronoun-confusion-sexual-fluidity.html.

BOSMAN, JULIE, AND MOTOKO RICH. "As Transgender Students Make Gains, Schools Hesitate at Bathrooms." *The New York Times*, 3 Nov. 2015, www.nytimes.com/2015/11/04/us/as-transgender-students-make-gains-schools

-hesitate-at-bathrooms.html.

Boylan, Jennifer Finney. "Trump's Contempt for Transgender Heroes." *The New York Times*, 26 July 2017, www.nytimes.com/2017/07/26/opinion/trumps-contempt-for-transgender-heroes.html.

Cacciola, Scott, and Alan Blinder. "N.B.A. to Move All-Star Game from North Carolina." *The New York Times*, 21 July 2016, www.nytimes.com/2016/07/22/sports/basketball/nba-all-star-game-moves-charlotte-transgender-bathroom-law.html.

Caron, Christina. "These Transgender Children Say They're Thriving. They Want to Help Others Do the Same." *The New York Times*, 20 Feb. 2018, www.nytimes.com/2018/02/20/us/gendercool-transgender.html.

Chokshi, Niraj. "Boy Scouts, Reversing Century-Old Stance, Will Allow Transgender Boys." *The New York Times*, 30 Jan. 2017, www.nytimes.com/2017/01/30/us/boy-scouts-reversing-century-old-stance-will-allow-transgender-boys.html.

Cooper, Helene. "Trump Cites Familiar Argument in Ban on Transgender Troops." *The New York Times*, 3 Aug. 2017, www.nytimes.com/2017/08/03/us/politics/transgender-military-trump.html.

Davis, Julie Hirschfeld, and Helene Cooper. "Trump Says Transgender People Will Not Be Allowed in the Military." *The New York Times*, 26 June 2017, www.nytimes.com/2017/07/26/us/politics/trump-transgender-military.html.

Davis, Julie Hirschfeld, and Matt Apuzzo. "U.S. Directs Public Schools to Allow Transgender Access to Restrooms." *The New York Times*, 12 May 2016, www.nytimes.com/2016/05/13/us/politics/obama-administration-to-issue-decree-on-transgender-access-to-school-restrooms.html.

Fernandez, Manny, and David Montgomery. "Texas Bathroom Bill Has Emotions, and Stakes, Running High." *The New York Times*, 21 June 2017, www.nytimes.com/2017/07/21/us/texas-bathroom-bill-transgender.html.

Grimm, Gavin. "Gavin Grimm: The Fight for Transgender Rights Is Bigger Than Me." *The New York Times*, 7 Mar. 2017, www.nytimes.com/2017/03/07/opinion/gavin-grimm-the-fight-for-transgender-rights-is-bigger-than-me.html.

Haberman, Clyde. "Beyond Caitlyn Jenner Lies a Long Struggle by Transgender People." *The New York Times*, 14 June 2015, www.nytimes.com/2015/06/15/us/beyond-caitlyn-jenner-lies-a-long-struggle-by-transgender-people.html.

Hartocollis, Anemona. "A Transgender Student Won Her Battle. Now It's

War." *The New York Times*, 2 Apr. 2017, www.nytimes.com/2017/04/02/us/transgender-students-township-illinois.html.

HARTOCOLLIS, ANEMONA. "Transgender Bathroom Debate Turns Personal at a Vermont High School." *The New York Times*, 17 May 2016, www.nytimes.com/2016/05/18/us/national-debate-over-transgender-bathrooms-turns-personal-at-rural-vermont-high-school.html.

HAUSER, CHRISTINE. "Transgender Directives for Schools Draw Reaction from Across the Country." *The New York Times*, 13 May 2016, www.nytimes.com/2016/05/14/us/transgender-students-and-new-rules-in-public-schools.html.

HEALY, JACK, AND RICHARD PÉREZ-PEÑA. "Solace and Fury as Schools React to Transgender Policy." *The New York Times*, 13 May 2016, www.nytimes.com/2016/05/14/us/transgender-bathrooms.html.

HOFFMAN, JAN. "Estimate of U.S. Transgender Population Doubles to 1.4 Million Adults." *The New York Times*, 30 June 2016, www.nytimes.com/2016/07/01/health/transgender-population.html.

JOHNSON, CYRÉE JARELLE. "Medicaid Work Requirements Are Yet Another Burden for Trans Workers." *The New York Times*, 5 Feb. 2018, www.nytimes.com/2018/02/05/opinion/medicaid-transgender-workers.html.

LICHTBLAU, ERIC, AND RICHARD FAUSSET. "U.S. Warns North Carolina That Transgender Bill Violates Civil Rights Laws." *The New York Times*, 4 May 2016, www.nytimes.com/2016/05/05/us/north-carolina-transgender-bathroom-bill.html.

LIPTAK, ADAM. "Supreme Court to Rule in Transgender Access Case." *The New York Times*, 28 Oct. 2016, www.nytimes.com/2016/10/29/us/politics/supreme-court-to-rule-in-transgender-access-case.html.

LIPTAK, ADAM. "Supreme Court Won't Hear Major Case on Transgender Rights." *The New York Times*, 6 Mar. 2017, www.nytimes.com/2017/03/06/us/politics/supreme-court-transgender-rights-case.html.

MANNING, CHELSEA. "Chelsea Manning: President Trump, Trans People in the Military Are Here to Stay." *The New York Times*, 27 July 2017, www.nytimes.com/2017/07/27/opinion/trump-transgender-military-chelsea-manning.html.

MAR, RIA TABACCO. "Trump Will Lose the Fight Over Bathrooms for Transgender Students." *The New York Times*, 23 Feb. 2017, www.nytimes.com/2017/02/23/opinion/trump-will-lose-the-fight-over-bathrooms-for-transgender-students.html.

MONTGOMERY, DAVID. "Texas Transgender Bathroom Bill Falters Amid Mounting Opposition." *The New York Times*, 8 Aug. 2017, www.nytimes.com/2017/08/16/us/politics/texas-bathroom-bill-dies-again-raising-republican-acrimony.html.

THE NEW YORK TIMES. "The Foolish Transgender Debate in Texas." *The New York Times*, 11 Aug. 2017, www.nytimes.com/2017/08/11/opinion/the-foolish-transgender-debate-in-texas.html.

THE NEW YORK TIMES. "How High School Students See the Transgender Bathroom Issue." *The New York Times*, 18 May 2016, www.nytimes.com/2016/05/19/us/high-school-students-transgender-bathroom.html.

THE NEW YORK TIMES. "Milestones in the American Transgender Movement." *The New York Times*, 28 Aug. 2015, www.nytimes.com/interactive/2015/05/15/opinion/editorial-transgender-timeline.html.

THE NEW YORK TIMES. "The Quest for Transgender Equality." *The New York Times*, 4 May 2015, www.nytimes.com/2015/05/04/opinion/the-quest-for-transgender-equality.html.

THE NEW YORK TIMES. "The Struggle for Fairness for Transgender Workers." *The New York Times*, 9 July 2015, www.nytimes.com/2015/07/09/opinion/the-struggle-for-fairness-for-transgender-workers.html.

THE NEW YORK TIMES. "For Transgender Americans, Legal Battles Over Restrooms." *The New York Times*, 27 July 2015, www.nytimes.com/2015/07/27/opinion/for-transgender-americans-legal-battles-over-restrooms.html.

THE NEW YORK TIMES. "Transgender Law Makes North Carolina Pioneer in Bigotry." *The New York Times*, 25 Mar. 2016, www.nytimes.com/2016/03/25/opinion/transgender-law-makes-north-carolina-pioneer-in-bigotry.html.

THE NEW YORK TIMES. "Transgender Troops Protected at Last." *The New York Times*, 30 June 2016, www.nytimes.com/2016/07/01/opinion/transgender-troops-protected-at-last.html.

PHILIPPS, DAVE. "Judge Blocks Trump's Ban on Transgender Troops in Military." *The New York Times*, 30 Oct. 2017, www.nytimes.com/2017/10/30/us/military-transgender-ban.html.

PHILIPPS, DAVE. "North Carolina Bans Local Anti-Discrimination Policies." *The New York Times*, 23 Mar. 2016, www.nytimes.com/2016/03/24/us/north-carolina-to-limit-bathroom-use-by-birth-gender.html.

PHILIPPS, DAVE. "For Transgender Service Members, a Mix of Sadness, Anger and Fear." *The New York Times*, 26 July 2017, www.nytimes.com/2017/07/26/us/for-transgender-service-members-a-mix-of-sadness-anger-and-fear.html.

REMNICK, NOAH. "Activists Say Police Abuse of Transgender People Persists

Despite Reforms." *The New York Times*, 6 Sept. 2015, www.nytimes.com/2015/09/07/nyregion/activists-say-police-abuse-of-transgender-people-persists-despite-reforms.html.

ROGERS, KATIE. "Seventeen Transgender Killings Contrast with Growing Visibility." *The New York Times*, 20 Aug. 2015, www.nytimes.com/2015/08/21/us/explosion-of-transgender-murders-contrast-with-growing-acceptance.html.

ROGERS, KATIE. "Transgender Students and 'Bathroom Laws' in South Dakota and Beyond." *The New York Times*, 25 Feb. 2016, www.nytimes.com/2016/02/26/us/transgender-students-and-bathroom-laws-in-south-dakota-and-beyond.html.

ROSENBERG, MATTHEW. "Transgender People Will Be Allowed to Serve Openly in Military." *The New York Times*, 30 June 2016, www.nytimes.com/2016/07/01/us/transgender-military.html.

SAVAGE, CHARLIE. "5 Transgender Service Members Sue Trump Over Military Ban." *The New York Times*, 9 Aug. 2017, www.nytimes.com/2017/08/09/us/politics/5-transgender-service-members-sue-trump-over-military-ban.html.

SIMS, JENNIFER. "I Am a Transgender Female Captain in the U.S. Army." *The New York Times*, 27 July 2017, www.nytimes.com/2017/07/27/opinion/trump-transgender-female-captain-army.html.

SMITH, MITCH. "South Dakota Bill on Transgender Students' Bathroom Access Draws Ire." *The New York Times*, 25 Feb. 2016, www.nytimes.com/2016/02/26/us/south-dakota-bill-on-transgender-students-bathroom-access-draws-ire.html.

STOLBERG, SHERYL GAY, ET AL. "How the Push to Advance Bathroom Rights for Transgender Americans Reached the White House." *The New York Times*, 21 May 2016, www.nytimes.com/2016/05/22/us/transgender-bathroom-obama-schools.html.

Index